"You may kiss the bride."

Mikolas revealed his bride's face and froze.

She was beautiful. Her mouth was eye-catching with a lush upper lip and a bashful bottom one tucked beneath it. Her chin was strong and came up a notch in a hint of challenge while her blue, blue irises blinked at him.

This was no girl on the brink of legal age. She was a woman, one who was mature enough to look him straight in the eye without flinching.

She was *not* Trina Stamos.

"Who the hell are you?"

Canadian **Dani Collins** knew in high school that she wanted to write romance for a living. Twenty-five years later, after marrying her high school sweetheart, having two kids with him, working at several generic office jobs and submitting countless manuscripts, she got "The Call." Her first Harlequin Presents novel won the Reviewers' Choice Award for Best First in Series from *RT Book Reviews*. She now works in her own office, writing romance.

Books by Dani Collins

Harlequin Presents

Bought by Her Italian Boss
Vows of Revenge
Seduced into the Greek's World
The Russian's Acquisition
An Heir to Bind Them
A Debt Paid in Passion
More than a Convenient Marriage?
No Longer Forbidden?

The Wrong Heirs

The Marriage He Must Keep
The Consequence He Must Claim

Seven Sexy Sins

The Sheikh's Sinful Seduction

The 21st Century Gentleman's Club

The Ultimate Seduction

One Night With Consequences

Proof of their Sin

Visit the Author Profile page at Harlequin.com for more titles.

Dani Collins

THE SECRET BENEATH
THE VEIL

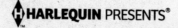

HARLEQUIN PRESENTS®

Recycling programs
for this product may
not exist in your area.

ISBN-13: 978-0-373-13468-7

The Secret Beneath the Veil

First North American publication 2016

Copyright © 2016 by Dani Collins

Printed in U.S.A.

THE SECRET BENEATH
THE VEIL

To you, Dear Reader, for loving romance novels as much as I do. I hope you enjoy this one.

masts bobbing on the water. Her sister was safe from this forced marriage to a stranger, she reminded herself, trying to calm her racing heart.

Forty minutes ago, Trina had let her father into the room where she was dressing. She'd still been wearing this gown, but hadn't yet put on the veil. She had promised Grigor she would be ready on time while Viveka had kept well out of sight. Grigor didn't even know Viveka was back on the island.

The moment he'd left the room, Viveka had helped Trina out of the gown and Trina had helped her into it. They had hugged hard, then Trina had disappeared down a service elevator and onto the seaplane her true love had chartered. They were making for one of the bigger islands to the north where arrangements were in place to marry them the moment they touched land. Viveka was buying them time by allaying suspicion, letting the ceremony continue as long as possible before she revealed herself and made her own escape.

She searched the horizon again, looking for the flag of the boat she'd hired. It was impossible to spot and that made her even more anxious than the idea of getting onto the perfectly serviceable craft. She hated boats, but she wasn't in the class that could afford private helicopters to take her to and fro. She'd given a sizable chunk of her savings to Stephanos, to help him spirit Trina away in that small plane. Spending the rest on crossing the Aegean in a speedboat was pretty close to her worst nightmare, but the ferry made only one trip per day and had left her here this morning.

She knew which slip the boat was using, though.

She'd paid the captain to wait and Stephanos had assured her she could safely leave her bags on board. Once she was exposed, she wouldn't even change. She would seek out that wretched boat, grit her teeth and sail into the sunset, content that she had finally prevailed over Grigor.

Her heart took a list and roll as they reached the top of the aisle, and Grigor handed her icy fingers to Trina's groom, the very daunting Mikolas Petrides.

His touch caused a *zing* of something to go through her. She told herself it was alarm. Nervous tension.

His grip faltered almost imperceptibly. Had he felt that static shock? His fingers shifted to enfold hers, pressing warmth through her whole body. Not comfort. She didn't fool herself into believing he would bother with that. He was even more intimidating in person than in his photos, exactly as Trina had said.

Viveka was taken aback by the quiet force he emanated, all chest and broad shoulders. He was definitely too much masculine energy for Viveka's little sister. He was too much for *her*.

She peeked into his face and found his gaze trying to penetrate the layers of her veil, brows lowered into sharp angles, almost as if he suspected the wrong woman stood before him.

Lord, he was handsome with those long clean-shaven plains below his carved cheekbones and the small cleft in his chin. His eyes were a smoky gray, outlined in black spiky lashes that didn't waver as he looked down his blade of a nose.

We could have blue-eyed children, she had thought

when she'd first clicked on his photo. It was one of those silly facts of genetics that had caught her imagination when she had been young enough to believe in perfect matches. To this day it was an attribute she thought made a man more attractive.

She had been tempted to linger over his image and speculate about a future with him, but she'd been on a mission from the moment Trina had tearfully told her she was being sold off in a business merger like sixteenth-century chattel. All Viveka had had to see were the headlines that tagged Trina's groom as the son of a murdered Greek gangster. No *way* would she let her sister marry this man.

Trina had begged Grigor to let her wait until March, when she turned eighteen, and to keep the wedding small and in Greece. That had been as much concession as he'd granted. Trina, legally allowed to marry whomever she wanted as of this morning, had *not* chosen Mikolas Petrides, wealth, power and looks notwithstanding.

Viveka swallowed. The eye contact seemed to be holding despite the ivory organza between them, creating a sense of connection that sent a fresh thrum of nervous energy through her system.

She and Trina both took after their mother in build, but Trina was definitely the darker of the two, with a rounder face and warm, brown eyes, whereas Viveka had these icy blue orbs and natural blond streaks she'd covered with the veil.

Did he know she wasn't Trina? She shielded her eyes with a drop of her lashes.

The shuffle of people sitting and the music halting sent a wash of perspiration over her skin. Could he hear her pulse slamming? Feel her trembles?

It's just a play, she reminded herself. Nothing about this was real or valid. It would be over soon and she could move on with her life.

At one time she had imagined acting for a living. All her early career ambitions had leaned toward starving artist of one kind or another, but she'd had to grow up fast and become more practical once her mother died. She had worked here at this yacht club, lying about her age so they'd hire her, washing dishes and scrubbing floors.

She had wanted to be independent of Grigor as soon as possible, away from his disparaging remarks that had begun turning into outright abuse. He had helped her along by kicking her out of the house before she'd turned fifteen. He'd kicked her off this island, really. Out of Greece and away from her sister because once he realized she had been working, that she had the means to support herself and wouldn't buckle to his will when he threatened to expel her from his home, he had ensured she was fired and couldn't get work anywhere within his reach.

Trina, just nine, had been the one to whisper, *Go. I'll be okay. You should go.*

Viveka had reached out to her mother's elderly aunt in London. She had known Hildy only from Christmas cards, but the woman had taken her in. It hadn't been ideal. Viveka got through it by dreaming of bringing her sister to live with her there. As recently as a few months ago, she had pictured them as two carefree young women, twenty-three and eighteen, figuring out their futures in the big city—

"I, Mikolas Petrides…"

He had an arresting voice. As he repeated his name and spoke his vows, the velvet-and-steel cadence of his tone held her. He smelled good, like fine clothes and spicy aftershave and something unique and masculine that she knew would imprint on her forever.

She didn't want to remember this for the rest of her life. It was a ceremony that wasn't even supposed to be happening. She was just a placeholder.

Silence made her realize it was her turn.

She cleared her throat and searched for a suitably meek tone. Trina had never been a target for Grigor. Not just because she was his biological daughter, but also because she was on the timid side—probably because her father was such a mean, loudmouthed, sexist bastard in the first place.

Viveka had learned the hard way to be terrified of Grigor. Even in London his cloud of intolerance had hung like a poison cloud, making her careful about when she contacted Trina, never setting Trina against him by confiding her suspicions, always aware he could hurt Viveka through her sister.

She had sworn she wouldn't return to Greece, certainly not with plans that would make Grigor hate her more than he already did, but she was confident he wouldn't do more than yell in front of all these wedding guests. There were media moguls in the assemblage and paparazzi circling the air and water.

The risk in coming here was a tall round of embarrassed confusion, nothing more.

She sincerely hoped.

The moment of truth approached. Her voice thinned and cracked, making her vows a credible imitation of Trina's as she spoke fraudulently in her sister's place, nullifying the marriage—and merger—that Grigor wanted so badly. It wasn't anything that could truly balance the loss of her mother, but it was a small retribution. Viveka wore a grim inner smile as she did it.

Her bouquet shook as she handed it off and her fingers felt clumsy and nerveless as she exchanged rings with Mikolas, keeping up the ruse right to the last minute. She wouldn't sign any papers, of course, and she would have to return these rings. Darn, she hadn't thought about that.

Even his hands were compelling, so well shaped and strong, so sure. One of his nails looked… She wasn't sure. Like he'd injured it once. If this were a real wedding, she would know that intimate detail about him.

Silly tears struck behind her eyes. She had the same girlish dreams for a fairy-tale wedding as any woman. She wished this were the beginning of her life with the man she loved. But it wasn't. Nothing about this was legal or real.

Everyone was about to realize that.

"You may kiss the bride."

Mikolas Petrides had agreed to this marriage for one reason only: his grandfather. He wasn't a sentimental man or one who allowed himself to be manipulated.

He sure as hell wasn't marrying for love. That word was an immature excuse for sex and didn't exist in the real world.

No, he felt nothing toward his bride. He felt nothing toward anyone, quite by conscious decision.

Even his loyalty to his grandfather was provisional. Pappoús had saved his life. He'd *given* Mikolas this life once their blood connection had been verified. He had recognized Mikolas as his grandson, pulling him from the powerless side of a brutal world to the powerful one.

Mikolas repaid him with duty and legitimacy. His grandfather had been born into a good family during hard times. Erebus Petrides hadn't stayed on the right side of the law as he'd done what he'd seen as necessary to survive. Living a corrupt life had cost the old man his son and Mikolas had been Erebus's second chance at an heir. He had given his grandson full rein with his ill-gotten empire on the condition Mikolas turn it into a legal—yet still lucrative—enterprise.

No small task, but this marriage merger was the final step. To the outside observer, Grigor's world-renowned conglomerate was absorbing a second-tier corporation with a questionable pedigree. In reality, Grigor was being paid well for a company logo. Mikolas would eventually run the entire operation.

Was it irony that his mother had been a laundress? Or appropriate?

Either way, this marriage had been Grigor's condition. He wanted his own blood to inherit his wealth. Mikolas had accepted to make good on his debt to his grandfather. Marriage would work for him in other ways and it was only another type of contract. This ceremony was more elaborate than most business meetings, but it was still just a date to fix signatures upon dotted lines followed by the requisite photo op.

Mikolas had met his bride—a girl, really—twice. She was young and extremely shy. Pretty enough, but no sparks of attraction had flared in him. He'd resigned himself to affairs while she grew up and they got to know one another. *Therein might be another advantage to marriage*, he had been thinking distantly, while he waited for her to walk down the aisle. Other women wouldn't wheedle for marriage if he already wore a ring.

Then her approach had transfixed him. Something happened. *Lust.*

He was never comfortable when things happened outside his control. This was hardly the time or place for a spike of naked hunger for a woman. But it happened.

She arrived before him veiled in a waterfall mist that he should have dismissed as an irritating affectation. For some reason he found the mystery deeply erotic. He recognized her perfume as the same scent she'd worn those other times, but rather than sweet and innocent, it now struck him as womanly and heady.

Her lissome figure wasn't as childish as he'd first judged, either. She moved as though she owned her body, and how had he not noticed before that her eyes were such a startling shade of blue, the kind that sat as a pool of water against a glacier? He could barely see her face, but the intensity of blue couldn't be dimmed by a few scraps of lace.

His heart began to thud with an old, painful beat. *Want*. The real kind. The kind that was more like basic necessity.

A flicker of panic threatened, but he clamped down on the memories of deprivation. Of denial. Terror. Searing pain.

He got what he wanted these days. Always. He was getting *her*.

Satisfaction rolled through him, filling him with anticipation for this pomp and circumstance to end.

The ceremony progressed at a glacial pace. Juvenile eagerness struck him when he was finally able to lift her veil. He didn't celebrate Christmas, yet felt it had arrived early, just for him.

He told himself it was gratification at accomplishing the goal his grandfather had assigned him. With this kiss, the balance sheets would come out of the rinse cycle, clean and pressed like new. Too bad the old man hadn't been well enough to travel here and enjoy this moment himself.

Mikolas revealed his bride's face and froze.

She was beautiful. Her mouth was eye-catching with a lush upper lip and a bashful bottom one tucked beneath it. Her chin was strong and came up a notch in a hint of challenge while her blue, blue irises blinked at him.

This was no girl on the brink of legal age. She was a woman, one who was mature enough to look him straight in the eye without flinching.

She was *not* Trina Stamos.

"Who the hell are you?"

Gasps went through the crowd.

The woman lifted a hand to brush her veil free of his dumbfounded fingers.

Behind her, Grigor shot to his feet with an ugly curse. "What are you doing here? Where's Trina?"

Yes. Where was his bride? Without the right woman here to speak her vows and sign her name, this marriage—*the merger*—was at a standstill. *No.*

As though she had anticipated Grigor's reaction, the bride zipped behind Mikolas, using him like a shield as the older man bore down on them.

"You little bitch!" Grigor hissed. Trina's father was not as shocked by the switch as he was incensed. He clearly knew this woman. A vein pulsed on his forehead beneath his flushed skin. "Where is she?"

Mikolas put up a hand, warding off the old man from grabbing the woman behind him. He would have his explanation from her before Grigor unleashed his temper.

Or maybe he wouldn't.

Another round of surprised gasps went through the crowd, punctuated by the clack of the fire door and a loud, repetitive ring of its alarm.

His bride had bolted out the emergency exit.

What the *hell*?

CHAPTER TWO

VIVEKA RAN EVERY DAY. She was fit and adrenaline pulsed through her arteries, giving her the ability to move fast and light as she fled Grigor and his fury.

The dress and the heels and the spaces between planks and the floating wharf were another story. *Bloody hell.*

She made it down the swaying ramp in one piece, thanks to the rails on either side, but then she was racing down the unsteady platform between the slips, scanning for the flag of her vessel—

The train of her dress caught. She didn't even see on what. She was yanked back and that was all it took for her to lose her footing completely. *Stupid heels.*

She turned her ankle, stumbled, tried to catch herself, hooked her toe in a pile of coiled rope and threw out an arm to snatch at the rail of the yacht in the slip beside her.

She missed, only crashing into the side of the boat with her shoulder. The impact made her "oof!" Her grasp was too little, too late. She slid sideways and would have screamed, but had the sense to suck in a big breath before she fell.

Cold, murky salt water closed over her.

Don't panic, she told herself, splaying out her limbs and only getting tangled in her dress and veil.

Mom. This was what it must have been like for her on that night far from shore, suddenly finding herself under cold, swirling water, tangled in an evening dress.

Don't panic.

Viveka's eyes stung as she tried to shift the veil enough to see which way the bubbles were going. Her dress hadn't stayed caught. It had come all the way in with her and floated all around her, obscuring her vision, growing heavier. The chill of the water penetrated to her skin. The weight of the dress dragged her down.

She kicked, but the layers of the gown were in the way. Her spiked heels caught in the fabric. This was futile. She was going to drown within swimming distance to shore. Grigor would stand above her and applaud.

The back of her hand scraped barnacles and her foot touched something. The seabed? Her hand burned where she'd scuffed it, but that told her there was a pillar somewhere here. She tried to scrabble her grip against it, desperately thinking she had never held her breath this long and couldn't hold it any longer.

Don't panic.

She clawed at her veil with her other hand, tried

to pull it off her hair. She would never get all these buttons open and the dress off in time to kick herself to the surface—

Don't panic.

The compulsion to gasp for air was growing unstoppable.

A hand grabbed her forearm and tugged her.

Yes, please. Oh, God, please!

Viveka blew out what little air she still had, fighting not to inhale, fighting to kick and help bring herself to the blur of light above her, fighting to reach it...

As she broke through, she gasped in a lungful of life-giving oxygen, panting with exertion, thrusting back her veil to stare at her rescuer.

Mikolas.

He looked murderous.

Her heart lurched.

With a yank, he dragged her toward a diving ramp off the back of a yacht and physically set her hand upon it. She slapped her other bleeding hand onto it, clinging for dear life. Oh, her hand stung. So did her lungs. Her stomach was knotted with shock over what had just happened. She clung to the platform with a death grip as she tried to catch her breath and think clear thoughts.

People were gathering along the slip, trying to see between the boats, calling to others in Greek and English. "There she is!" "He's got her." "They're safe."

Viveka's dress felt like it was made of lead. It continued trying to pull her under, tugged by the wake

that set all the boats around them rocking and sucking. She shakily managed to scrape the veil off her
hair, ignoring the yank on her scalp as she raked it
from her head. She let it float away, not daring to look
for Grigor. She'd caught a glimpse of his stocky legs
and that was enough. Her heart pounded in reaction.

"What the *hell* is going on?" Mikolas said in that
darkly commanding voice. "Where is Trina? Who
are you?"

"I'm her sis—" Viveka took a mouthful of water
as a swell bashed the boat they clung to. "*Pah.* She
didn't want to marry you."

"Then she shouldn't have agreed to." He hauled
himself up to sit on the platform.

Oh, yes, it was just that easy.

He was too hard to face with that lethal expression.
How did he manage to look so action-star handsome
with his white shirt plastered to his muscled shoulders, his coat and tie gone, his hair flattened to his
head? It was like staring into the sun.

Viveka looked out to where motorboats had circled
to see where the woman in the wedding gown had
fallen into the water.

Was that her boat? She wanted to wave, but kept
a firm grip on the yacht as she used her free hand to
pick at the buttons on her back. She eyed the distance
to the red-and-gold boat. She couldn't swim that far in
this wretched dress, but if she managed to shed it...?

Mikolas stood and, without asking, bent down to
grasp her by the upper arms, pulling her up and out
of the water, grunting loud enough that it was insult-

ing. He swore after landing her on her feet beside
him. His chest heaved while he glared at her limp,
stained gown.

Viveka swayed on her feet, trying to keep her balance as the yacht rocked beneath them. She was still
wearing the ridiculously high heels, was still in shock,
but for a few seconds she could only stare at Mikolas.

He had saved her life.

No one had gone out of their way to help her like
that since her mother was alive. She'd been a pariah
to Grigor and a burden on her aunt, mostly fending
for herself since her mother's death.

She swallowed, trying to assimilate a deep and
disturbing gratitude. She had grown a thick shell that
protected her from disregard, but she didn't know how
to deal with kindness. She was moved.

Grigor's voice above her snapped her back to her
situation. She had to get away. She yanked at her
bodice, tearing open the delicate buttons on her spine
and trying to push the clinging fabric down her hips.

She wore only a white lace bra and underpants beneath, but that was basically a bikini. Good enough
to swim out to her getaway craft.

To her surprise, Mikolas helped her, rending the
gown as if he cursed its existence, leaving it puddled
around her feet and sliding into the water. He didn't
give her a chance to dive past him, however. He set
wide hands on her waist and hefted her upward where
bruising hands took hold of her arms—

Grigor.

"Nooo!" she screamed.

* * *

That ridiculous woman nearly kicked him in the face as he hefted her off the diving platform to the main deck of the yacht. Grigor was above, taking hold of her to bring her up. What did she think? That he was throwing her back into the sea?

"Noooo!" she cried and struggled, but Grigor pulled her all the way onto the deck where he stood.

She must be crazy, behaving like this.

Mikolas came up the ladder with the impetus of a man taking charge. He hated surprises. *He* controlled what happened to himself. No one else.

At least Grigor hadn't set this up. He'd been tricked as well, or he wouldn't be so furious.

Mikolas was putting that together as he came up to see Grigor shaking the nearly naked woman like a terrier with a rat. Then he slapped her across the face hard enough to send her to her knees.

No stranger to violence, Mikolas still took it like a punch to the throat. It appalled him on a level so deep he reacted on blind instinct, grabbing Grigor's arm and shoving him backward even as the woman threw up her arm as though to block a kick.

Stupid reaction, he thought distantly. It was a one-way ticket to a broken forearm.

But now was not the moment for a tutorial on street fighting.

Grigor found his balance and trained his homicidal gaze on Mikolas.

Mikolas centered his balance with readiness, but in his periphery saw the woman stagger toward the rail. Oh, hell, no. She was not going to ruin his day, then slip away like a siren into the deep.

He turned from Grigor's bitter "You should have let her drown" and provoked a cry of "Put me down!" from the woman as he caught her up against his chest.

She was considerably lighter without the gown, but still a handful of squirming damp skin and slippery muscle as he carried her off the small yacht.

On the pier, people parted and swiveled like gaggles of geese, some dressed in wedding regalia, others obviously tourists and sailors, all babbling in different languages as they took in the commotion.

It was a hundred meters to his own boat and he felt every step, thanks to the pedal of the woman's sharp, silver heels.

"Calm yourself. I've had it with this sideshow. You're going to tell me where my bride has gone and why."

CHAPTER THREE

VIVEKA WAS SHAKING right down to her bones. Grigor had hit her, right there in front of the whole world. Well, the way the yacht had been positioned, only Mikolas had probably seen him, but in the back of her mind she was thinking that this was the time to call the police. With all these witnesses, they couldn't ignore her complaint. Not this time.

Actually, they probably could. Her report of assault and her request for a proper investigation into her mother's death had never been heeded. The officers on this island paid rent to Grigor and didn't like to impact their personal lives by carrying out their sworn duties. She had learned that bitter lesson years ago.

And this brute wouldn't let her go to do anything!

He was really strong. He carried her in arms that were so hard with steely muscle it almost hurt to be held by them. She could tell it wasn't worth wasting her energy trying to escape. And he wore a mask of such controlled fury he intimidated her.

She instinctively drew in on herself, stomach

churning with reaction while her brain screamed at her to swim out to her hired boat.

"Let me go," she insisted in a more level tone.

Mikolas only bit out orders for ice and bandages to a uniformed man as he carried her up a narrow gangplank, boarding a huge yacht of aerodynamic layers and spaceship-like rigging. The walls were white, the decks teak, the sheer size and luxury of the vessel making it more like a cruise liner than a personal craft.

Greek mafia, she thought, and wriggled harder, signaling that she sincerely wanted him to put her down. *Now.*

Mikolas strode into what had to be the master cabin. She caught only a glimpse of its grand decor before he carried her all the way into a luxurious en suite and started the shower.

"Warm up," he ordered and pointed to the black satin robe on the back of the door. "Then we'll bandage your hand and ice your face while you explain yourself."

He left.

She snorted. *Not likely.*

Folding her arms against icy shivers, she eyed the small porthole that looked into the expanse of open water beyond the marina. She might fit through it, but even as the thought formed, a crewman walked by on the deck outside. She would be discovered before she got through it and in any case, she wasn't up for another swim. Not yet. She was trembling.

Reaction was setting in. She had nearly drowned.

Grigor had hit her. He'd do worse if he got his hands on her again. Had he come aboard behind them?

She wanted to cry out of sheer, overwhelmed reaction.

But she wouldn't.

Trina was safe, she reminded herself. Never again did she have to worry about her little sister. Not in the same way, anyway.

The steaming shower looked incredibly inviting. Its gentle hiss beckoned her.

Don't cry, she warned herself, because showers were her go-to place for letting emotion overcome her, but she couldn't afford to let down her guard. She may yet have to face Grigor again.

Her insides congealed at the thought.

She would need to pull herself together for that, she resolved, and closed the curtain across the porthole before picking herself free of the buckles on her shoes. She stepped into the shower still wearing her bra and undies, then took them off to rinse them and— Oh. She let out a huff of faint laughter as she saw her credit card stuck to her breast.

The chuckle was immediately followed by a stab of concern. Her bags, passport, phone and purse were on the hired boat. Was the captain waiting a short trot down the wharf? Or bobbing out in the harbor, wondering if she'd drowned? Grabbing this credit card and shoving it into her bra had been a last-minute insurance against being stuck without resources if things went horribly wrong, but she hadn't imagined things would go *this* far wrong.

The captain was waiting for her, she assured herself. She would keep her explanations short and sweet to Mikolas and be off. He seemed like a reasonable man.

She choked on another snort of laughter, this one edging toward hysteria.

Then another wave of that odd defenselessness swirled through her. Why had Mikolas saved her? It made her feel like— She didn't know what this feeling was. She never relied on anyone. She'd never been *able* to. Her mother had loved her, but she'd died. Trina had loved her, but she'd been too young and timorous to stand up to Grigor. Aunt Hildy had helped her to some extent, but on a quid-pro-quo basis.

Mikolas was a stranger who had risked his life to preserve hers. She didn't understand it.

It infused her with a sense that she was beholden to him. She hated that feeling. She had had a perfect plan to get Hildy settled, bring Trina to London once she was eighteen and finally start living life on her own terms. Then Grigor had ruined it by promising Trina to this...*criminal*.

A criminal who wasn't averse to fishing a woman out of the sea—something her stepfather hadn't bothered doing with her mother, leaving that task to search and rescue.

She was still trembling, still trying to make sense of it as she dried off with a thick black towel monogrammed with a silver *M*. She stole a peek in his medicine chest, bandaged her hand, used some kind of man-brand moisturizer that didn't have a scent, rinsed with his mouthwash, then untangled her hair with a comb that smelled like his shampoo. She used his hair dryer to dry her underwear and put both back on under his robe.

The robe felt really good, light and cool and slippery against her humid skin.

She felt like his lover wearing something this intimate.

The thought made her blush and a strange wistfulness hit her as she worked off his rings—both the diamond that Trina had given her and the platinum band he'd placed on her finger himself—and set them on the hook meant for facecloths. He was *not* the sort of man she would ever want to marry. He was far too daunting and she needed her independence, but she did secretly long for someone to share her life with. Someone kind and tender who would make her laugh and maybe bring her flowers sometimes.

Someone who wanted her in his life.

She would *not* grow maudlin about her sister running off with Stephanos, seemingly choosing him over Viveka, leaving her nursing yet another sting of rejection. Her sister was entitled to fall in love.

With a final deep breath, she emerged into the stateroom.

Mikolas was there, wearing a pair of black athletic shorts and towel-dried hair, nothing else. His silhouette was a bleak, masculine statue against the closed black curtains.

The rest of the room was surprisingly spacious for a boat, she noted with a sweeping glance. There was a sitting area with a comfortable-looking sectional facing a big-screen TV. A glass-enclosed office allowed a tinted view of a private deck in the bow. She averted her gaze from the huge bed covered with a black satin spread and came back to the man who watched her with an indecipherable expression.

He held a drink, something clear and neat. Ouzo, she assumed. His gaze snagged briefly on the red mark on her cheek before traversing to her bare feet and coming back to slam into hers.

His expression still simmered with anger, but there was something else that took her breath. A kind of male assessment that signaled he was weighing her as a potential sex partner.

Involuntarily, she did the same thing. How could she not? He was really good-looking. His build was amazing, from those broad, bare shoulders to that muscled chest to those washboard abs and soccer-star legs.

She was not a woman who gawked at men. She considered herself a feminist and figured if it was tasteless for men to gaze at pinup calendars, then women shouldn't objectify men, either, but seriously. *Wow.* He was muscly without being overdeveloped. His skin was toasted a warm brown and that light pattern of hair on his chest looked like it had been sculpted by the loving hand of Mother Nature, not any sort of waxing specialist.

An urge to touch him struck her. Sexual desire wasn't something that normally hit her out of the blue like this, but she found herself growing warm with more than embarrassment. She wondered what it would be like to roam her mouth over his torso, to tongue his nipples and lick his skin. She felt an urge to splay her hands over his muscled waist and explore lower, push aside his waistband and *possess*.

Coils of sexual need tightened in her belly.

Where was the lead-up? The part where she spent ages kissing and nuzzling before she decided maybe she'd like to take things a little further? She never flashed to shoving down a man's pants and stroking him!

But that fantasy hit her along with a deep yearning and a throbbing pinch between her legs.

Was he getting *hard*? The front of his shorts lifted.

She realized where her gaze had fixated and jerked her eyes back to his, shocked with herself and at his blatant reaction.

His expression was arrested, yet filled with consideration and—she caught her breath—yes, that was an invitation. An arrogant *Help yourself.* Along with something predatory. Something that was barely contained. Decision. Carnal hunger.

The air grew so sexually charged, she couldn't find oxygen in it. The rhythm of her breaths changed, becoming subtle pants. Her nipples were stimulated by the shift of the robe against the lace of her bra. She became both wary and meltingly receptive.

This was crazy. She shook her head, as if she could erase all this sexual tension like an app that erased content on her phone if she joggled it back and forth hard enough.

With monumental effort, she jerked her gaze from his and stared blindly at the streak of light between the curtains. She folded her arms in self-protection and kept him in her periphery.

This was really stupid, letting him bring her into his bedroom like this. A single woman who lived in the city knew to be more careful.

"Use the ice," he said with what sounded like a hint of dry laughter in his tone. He nodded toward a side table where an ice pack sat on a small bar towel.

"It's not that bad," she dismissed. She'd had worse. Her lip might be puffed a little at the corner, but it was nothing like the time she'd walked around with a huge black eye, barely able to see out of it, openly telling people that Grigor had struck her. *You shouldn't talk back to him*, her teacher had said, mouth tight, gaze avoiding hers.

Grigor shouldn't have called her a whore and burned all her photos of her mother, she had retorted, but no one had wanted to hear *that*.

Mikolas didn't say anything, only came toward her, making her snap her head around and warn him off with a look.

Putting his glass down, he lifted his phone and clicked, taking a photo of her, surprising her so much she scowled.

"What are you doing?"

"Documenting. I assume Grigor will claim you were hurt falling into the water," he advised with cool detachment.

"You don't want me to try to discredit your business partner? Is that what you're saying? Are you going to take a photo after you leave your own mark on the other side of my face?" It was a dicey move, daring him like that, but she was so *sick* of people protecting *Grigor*. And she needed to know Mikolas's intentions, face them head-on.

Mikolas's stony eyes narrowed. "I don't hit women." His mouth pulled into a smile that was more an expression of lethal power than anything else. "And Grigor has discredited himself." He tilted the phone to indicate the photo. "Which may prove useful."

Viveka's insides tightened as she absorbed how cold-blooded that was.

"I didn't know Grigor had another daughter." Mikolas moved to take up his drink again. "Do you want one?" he asked, glancing toward the small wet bar next to the television. Both were inset against the shiny wood-grain cabinetry.

She shook her head. Better to keep her wits.

"Grigor isn't my father." She always took great satisfaction in that statement. "My mother married him when I was four. She died when I was nine. He doesn't talk about her, either."

Or the boating accident. Her heart clenched like a fist, trying to hang on to her memories of her mother, knotting in fury at the lack of a satisfactory explanation, wanting to beat the truth from Grigor if she had to.

"Do you have a name?" he asked.

"Viveka." The corner of her mouth pulled as she

realized they'd come this far without it. She was practically naked, wearing a robe that had brushed his own skin and surrounded her in the scent of his aftershave. "Brice," she added, not clarifying that most people called her Vivi.

"Viveka," he repeated, like he was trying out the sound. They were speaking English and his thick accent gave an exotic twist to her name as he shaped out the *Vive* and added a short, hard *ka* to the end.

She licked her lips, disturbed by how much she liked the way he said it.

"Why the melodrama, Viveka? I asked your sister if she was agreeable to this marriage. She said yes."

"Do you think she would risk saying no to something Grigor wanted?" She pointed at the ache on her face.

Mikolas's expression grew circumspect as he dropped his gaze into his drink, thumb moving on the glass. It was the only indication his thoughts were restless beneath that rock-face exterior.

"If she wants more time," he began.

"She's marrying someone else," she cut in. "Right this minute, if all has gone to plan." She glanced for a clock, but didn't see one. "She knew Stephanos at school and he worked on Grigor's estate as a landscaper."

Trina had loved the young man from afar for years, never wanting to tip her hand to Grigor by so much as exchanging more than a shy hello with Stephanos, but she had waxed poetic to Viveka on dozens of occasions. Viveka hadn't believed Stephanos returned the crush until Trina's engagement to Mikolas had been announced.

"When Stephanos heard she was marrying someone else, he asked Trina to elope. He has a job outside of Athens." One that Grigor couldn't drop the ax upon.

"Weeding flower beds?" Mikolas swirled his drink. "She could have kept him on the side after we married, if that's what she wanted."

"Really," Viveka choked.

He shrugged a negligent shoulder. "This marriage is a business transaction, open to negotiation. I would have given her children if she wanted them, or a divorce eventually, if that was her preference. She should have spoken to me."

"Because you're such a reasonable man—who just happens to trade women like stocks and bonds."

"I'm a man who gets what he wants," he said in a soft voice, but it was positively deadly. "I want this merger."

He sounded so merciless her heart skipped in alarm. *Gangster.* She found a falsely pleasant smile.

"I wish you great success in making your dreams come true. Do you mind if I wear this robe to my boat? I can bring it back after I dress or maybe one of your staff could come with me?" She pushed her hand into the pocket and gripped her credit card, feeling the edge dig into her palm. Where was Grigor? she wondered. She had no desire to pass him on the dock and get knocked into the water again—this time unconscious.

Mikolas's expression didn't change. He said nothing, but she had the impression he was laughing at her again.

Something made her look toward the office and the view beyond the bow. The marina was tucked against a very small indent on the island's coastline. The view from shore was mostly an expanse of the Aegean. But the boats weren't passing in front of this craft. They were coming and going on both sides. The slant of sunlight on the water had shifted.

The yacht was moving.

"Are you kidding me?" she screeched.

CHAPTER FOUR

MIKOLAS THREW BACK the last of his ouzo, clenched his
teeth against the burn and set aside his glass with a
decisive *thunk*. He searched for the void that he usually occupied, but he couldn't find it. He was swirling
in a miasma of lascivious need, achingly hard after
the way Viveka had stared at his crotch and swallowed like her mouth was watering.

He absently ran a hand across his chest where his
nipples were so sharp they pained him and adjusted
himself so he wouldn't pop out of his shorts, resisting
the urge to soothe the ache with a squeeze of his fist.

His reaction to her was unprecedented. He was an
experienced man, had a healthy appetite for sex, but
had never reacted so immediately and irrepressibly
to any woman.

This lack of command over himself disturbed him.
Infuriated him. He was insulted at being thrown over
for a gardener and unclear on his next move. Retreat
was never an option for him, but he'd left the island
to regroup. That smacked of cowardice and he pinned
the blame for all of it on this woman.

While she stood there with her hand closed over the lapels of his robe, holding it tight beneath her throat. Acting virginal when she was obviously as wily and experienced as any calculating opportunist he'd ever met.

"Let's negotiate our terms, Viveka." From the moment she had admitted to being Trina's sister he had seen the logical way to rescue this deal. Hell, by turning up in Trina's gown she'd practically announced to him how this would play out.

Of course it was a catch-22. He wasn't sure he wanted such a tempting woman so close to him, but he refused to believe she was anything he couldn't handle.

Viveka only flashed him a disparaging look and spun toward the door.

He didn't bother stopping her. He followed at a laconic pace as she scurried her way out to the stern of the mid-deck. Grasping the rail in one hand, she shaded her eyes with the other, scanning the empty horizon. She quickly threw herself to the port side. Gazing back to the island, which had been left well behind them, she made a distressed noise and glared at him again, expression white.

"Is Grigor on board?"

"Why would he be?"

"I don't know!" Her shoulders relaxed a notch, but she continued to look anxious. "Why did you leave the island?"

"Why would I stay?"

"Why would you take me?" she cried.

"I want to know why you've taken your sister's place."

"You didn't have to leave shore for that!"

"You wanted Grigor present? He seemed to be inflaming things." Grigor hadn't expected his departure, either. Mikolas's phone had already buzzed several times with calls from his would-be business partner.

That had been another reason for Mikolas's departure. If he'd stayed, he might have assaulted Grigor. The white-hot urge had been surprisingly potent and yes, that too had been provoked by this exasperating woman.

It wasn't a desire to protect *her*, Mikolas kept telling himself. His nature demanded he dominate, particularly over bullies and brutes. His personal code of ethics wouldn't allow him to stand by and watch any man batter a woman.

But Grigor's attack on this one had triggered something dark and primal in him, something he didn't care to examine too closely. Since cold-blooded murder was hardly a walk down the straight and narrow that was his grandfather's expectation of him, he'd taken himself out of temptation's reach.

"I had a boat hired! All my things are on it." Viveka pointed at the island. "Take me back!"

Such a bold little thing. Time to let her know who was boss.

"Grigor promised this merger if I married his daughter." He gave her a quick once-over. "His stepdaughter will do."

She threw back her head. "Ba-ha-ha," she near shouted and shrugged out of his robe, dropping it to the deck. "No. 'Bye." Something flashed in her hand as she started to climb over the rail.

She was fine-boned and supple and so easy to take in hand. Perhaps he took more enjoyment than he should in having another reason to touch her. Her skin was smooth and warm, her wrists delicate in his light grip as he calmly forced them behind her back, trapping her between the rail and his body.

She strained to look over her shoulder, muttering, "Oh, you—!" as something fell into the water with a glint of reflected light. "That was my credit card. Thanks a *lot*."

"Viveka." He was stimulated by the feel of her naked abdomen against his groin, erection not having subsided much and returning with vigor. Her spiked heels were gone, which was a pity. They'd been sexy as hell, but when it came to rubbing up against a woman, the less clothes the better.

She smelled of his shampoo, he noted, but there was an intriguing underlying scent that was purely hers: green tea and English rain. And that heady scent went directly into his brain, numbing him to everything but thoughts of being inside her.

Women were more subtle than men with their responses, but he read hers as clearly as a billboard. Not just the obvious signs like the way her nipples spiked against the pattern of her see-through bra cups, erotically abrading his chest and provoking thoughts of licking and sucking at them until she squirmed and moaned. A blush stained her cheeks and she licked her lips. There was a bonelessness to her. He could practically feel the way her blood moved through her veins like warm honey. He knew instinctively that opening his mouth against her neck would make her shiver and surrender to him. Her arousal would feed into his and they'd take each other to a new dimension.

Where did that ridiculous notion come from? He was no sappy poet. He tried to shake the idea out of his head, but couldn't rid himself of the certainty that sex with her would be the best he'd ever known. They were practically catching fire from this light friction. His heart was ramping with strength in his chest, his body magnetized to hers.

He was incensed with her, he reminded himself, but he was also intrigued by this unique attunement they had. Logic told him it was dangerous, but the primitive male inside him didn't give a damn. He *wanted* her.

"This is kidnapping. And assault," she said, giving a little struggle against his grip. "I thought you didn't hurt women."

"I don't let them hurt themselves, either. You'll kill yourself jumping into the water out here."

Something flickered in her expression. Her skin was very white compared with her sister's. How had he not noticed that from the very first, veil notwithstanding?

"Stop behaving like a spoiled child," he chided.

She swung an affronted look to him like it was the

worst possible insult he could level at her. "How about you stop acting like you own the world?"

"This *is* my world. You walked into it. Don't complain how I run it."

"I'm trying to leave it."

"And I'll let you." Something twisted in his gut, as if that was a lie. A big one. "After you fix the damage you've done."

"How do you suggest I do that?"

"Marry me in your sister's place."

She made a choking noise and gave another wriggle of protest, heel hooking on the lower rung of the rail as if she thought she could lift herself backward over the rail.

All she managed to do was pin herself higher against him. She stilled. Hectic color deepened in her cheekbones.

He smiled, liking what she'd done. Her movement had opened her legs and brought her cleft up to nestle against his shaft. She'd caught the same zing of sexual excitement that her movement had sent through him. He nudged lightly, more of a tease than a threat, and watched a delicate shiver go through her.

It was utterly enthralling. He could only stare at her parted, quivering mouth. He wanted to cover and claim it. He wanted to drag his tongue over every inch of her. Wanted to push at his elastic waistband, press aside that virginal white lace and thrust into the heat that was branding him through the thin layers between them.

He had expected to spend this week frustrated.

Now he began to forgive her for this switch of hers. They would do very nicely together. Very. Nicely.

"Let's take this back to my stateroom." His voice emanated from somewhere deep in his chest, thick with the desire that gripped him.

Her eyes flashed with fear before she said tautly, "To consummate a marriage that won't happen? Did you see how Grigor reacted to me? He'll never let me sub in for Trina. If anything would make him refuse your merger, marrying me would do it."

Mikolas slowly relaxed his grip and stepped back, trailing light fingers over the seams at her hips.

Goose bumps rose all over her, but she ignored it, hoping her knickers weren't showing the dampness that had released at the feel of him pressed against her.

What was *wrong* with her? She didn't even *do* sex. Kissing and petting were about it.

She dipped to pick up the robe and knotted it with annoyance. How could she be this hot when the wind had cooled to unpleasant and the sky was thickening with clouds?

She sent an anxious look at the ever-shrinking island amid the growing whitecaps. It was way too far to swim. Mikolas might have done her a favor taking her out of Grigor's reach, but being at sea thinned her composure like it was being spun out from a spool.

"You're saying if I want Grigor to go through with the merger, I should turn you over to him?" he asked.

"What? *No!*" Such terror slammed into her, her

knees nearly buckled. "Why would you even think of doing something like that?"

"The merger is important to me."

"My *life* is important to me." Tears stung her eyes and she had to blink hard to be able to see him. She had a feeling her lips were trembling. Where was the man who had saved her? Right now, Mikolas looked as conscienceless as Grigor.

Crushed to see that indifference, she hid her distress by averting her gaze and swallowed back the lump in her throat.

"This is nothing," she said with as much calm as she could, pointing at her face, trying to reach through to the man who had said he didn't hurt women. "Barely a starting point for him. I'd rather take my chances with the sharks."

"You already have." The flatness of his voice sent a fresh quake of uncertainty through her center.

What did it say about how dire her situation was that she was searching for ways to reach him? To persuade *this* shark to refrain from offering her gift-wrapped to the other one?

"If—if—" She wasn't really going to say this, was she? She briefly hung her head, but what choice did she have? She didn't have to go all the way, just make it good for him, right? She had a little experience with that. A very tiny little bit. He was hard, which meant he was up for it, right? "If you want sex…"

He made a scoffing noise. "*You* want sex. I'll decide if and when I give it to you. There's no leverage in offering it to me."

Sex was a basket of hang-ups for her. Offering herself had been really hard. Now she felt cheap and useless.

She pushed her gaze into the horizon, trying to hide how his denigration carved into her hard-won confidence.

"Go below," he commanded. "I want to make some calls."

She went because she needed to be away from him, needed to lick her wounds and reassess.

A purser showed her into a spacious cabin with a sitting room, a full en suite and a queen bed with plenty of tasseled pillows in green and gold. The cabinetry was polished to showcase the artistic grains in the amber-colored wood and the room was well-appointed with cosmetics, fresh fruit, champagne and flowers.

Her stomach churned too much to even think of eating, but she briefly considered drinking herself into oblivion. Once she noticed the laptop dock, however, she began looking for a device to contact... whom? Aunt Hildy wasn't an option. Her workmates might pick up a coffee or cover for her if she had to run home, but that was the extent of favors she could ask of them.

It didn't matter anyway. There was nothing here. The telephone connected to the galley or the bridge. The television was part of an onboard network that could be controlled by a tablet, but there was no tablet to be found.

At least she came across clothes. Women's, she

noted with a cynical snort. Mikolas must have been planning to keep his own paramour on the side after his marriage.

Everything was in Viveka's size, however, and it struck her that this was Trina's trousseau. This was her sister's suite.

Mikolas hadn't expected her sister to share his room? Did that make him more hard-hearted than she judged him? Or less?

Men never dominated her thoughts this way. She never let them make her feel self-conscious and second-guess every word that passed between them. This obsession with Mikolas was a horribly susceptible feeling, like he was important to her when he wasn't.

Except for the fact he held her life in his iron fist.

Thank God she had saved Trina from marrying him. She'd done the right thing taking her sister's place and didn't hesitate to make herself at home among her things, weirdly comforted by a sense of closeness to her as she did.

Pulling on a floral wrap skirt and a peasant blouse—both deliberately light and easily removed if she happened to find herself treading water—Viveka had to admit she was relieved Mikolas had stopped her from jumping. She *would* rather take her chances with sharks than with Grigor, but she didn't have a death wish. She was trying not to think of her near drowning earlier, but it had scared the hell out of her.

So did the idea of being sent back to Grigor.

Somehow she had to keep a rational head, but after leaving Grigor's oppression and withstanding Aunt Hildy's virulence, Viveka couldn't take being subjugated anymore. That's why she'd come back to help Trina make her own choices. The idea of her sister living in sufferance as part of a ridiculous business deal had made her furious!

Opening the curtains that hid two short, wide portholes stacked upon each other, she searched the horizon for a plan. At least this wasn't like that bouncy little craft she'd dreaded. This monstrosity moved more smoothly and quietly than the ferry. It might even take her to Athens.

That would work, she decided. She would ask Mikolas to drop her on the mainland. She would meet up with Trina, Stephanos could arrange for her things to be delivered, and she would find her way home.

This pair of windows was some sort of extension, she realized, noting the cleverly disguised seam between the upper and lower windows. The top would lift into an awning while the bottom pushed out to become the railing on a short balcony. Before she thought it through, her finger was on the button next to the diagram.

The wall began to crack apart while an alarm went off with a horrible honking blare, scaring her into leaping back and swearing aloud.

Atop that shock came the interior door slamming open.

Mikolas had dressed in suit pants and a crisp white shirt and wore a *terrible* expression.

* * *

"I just wanted to see what it did!" Viveka cried, holding up a staying hand.

What a liability she was turning into.

Mikolas moved to stop and reverse the extension of the balcony while he sensed the engines being cut and the yacht slowing. As the wall restored itself, he picked up the phone and instructed his crew to stay the course.

Hanging up, he folded his arms and told himself this rush of pure, sexual excitement each time he looked at Viveka was transitory. It was the product of a busy few weeks when he hadn't made time for women combined with his frustration over today's events. Of course he wanted to let off steam in a very base way.

She delivered a punch simply by standing before him, however. He had to work at keeping his thoughts from conjuring a fantasy of removing that village girl outfit of hers. The wide, drawstring collar where her bra strap peeked was an invitation, the bare calves beneath the hem of her pretty skirt a promise of more silken skin higher up.

Those unpainted toes seemed ridiculously unguarded. So did the rest of her, with her hair tied up like a teenager and her face clean.

Some women used makeup as war paint, others as an invitation. Viveka hadn't used any. She hadn't tried to cover the bruise, and lifted that discolored, belligerent chin of hers in a brave stare that was utterly foolish. She had no idea whom she was dealing with.

Yet something twisted in his chest. He found her nerve entirely too compelling. He wanted to feed that spark of energy and watch it detonate in his hands. He bet she scratched in bed and was dismayingly eager to find out.

Women were *never* a weakness for him. No one was. Nothing. Weakness was abhorrent to him. Helplessness was a place he refused to revisit.

"We'll eat." He swept a hand to where the door was still open and one of the porters hovered.

He sent the man to notify the chef and steered her to the upper aft deck. The curved bench seat allowed them to slide in from either side, shifting cushions until they met in the middle, where they looked out over the water. Here the wind was gentled by the bulk of the vessel. It was early spring so the sun was already setting behind the clouds on the horizon.

She cast a vexed look toward the view. He took it as annoyance that the island was long gone behind them and privately smirked, then realized she was doing it again: pulling all his focus and provoking a reaction in him.

He forced his attention to the porter as he arrived with place settings and water.

"You'll eat seafood?" he said to Viveka as the porter left.

"If you tell me to, of course I will."

A rush of anticipation for the fight went through him. "Save your breath," he told her. "I don't shame."

"How does someone influence you, then? Money?" She affected a lofty tone, but quit fiddling with her silverware and tucked her hands in her lap, turning her head to read him. "Because I would like to go to Athens—as opposed to wherever you think you're taking me."

"I have money," he informed, skipping over what he intended to do next because he was still deciding.

He stretched out his arms so his left hand, no longer wearing the ring she'd put on it, settled behind her shoulder. He'd put the ring in his pocket along with the ones she had worn. Her returning them surprised him. She must have known what they were worth. Why wasn't she trying to use them as leverage? Not that it would work, but he expected a woman in her position to at least try.

He dismissed that puzzle and returned to her question. "If someone wants to influence me, they offer something I want."

"And since I don't have anything you want…?" Little flags of color rose on her cheekbones and she stared out to sea.

He almost smiled, but the tightness of her expression caused him to sober. Had he hurt her with his rejection earlier? He'd been brutal because he wasn't a novice. You didn't enter into any transaction wearing your desires on your sleeve the way she did.

But how could she not be aware that she *was* something he wanted? Did she not feel the same pull he was experiencing?

How did she keep undermining his thoughts this way?

As an opponent she was barely worth noticing. A

brief online search had revealed she had no fortune, no influence. Her job was a pedestrian position as data entry clerk for an auto parts chain. Her network of social media contacts was small, which suggested an even smaller circle of real friends.

Mikolas's instinct when attacked was to crush. If Grigor had switched his bride on purpose, he would already be ruined. Mikolas didn't lose to anyone, especially weak adversaries who weren't even big enough to appear on his radar.

Yet Viveka had slipped in like a ninja, taking him unawares. On the face of it, that made her his enemy. He had to treat her with exactly as much detachment as he would any other foe.

But this twist of hunger in his gut demanded an answering response from her. It wasn't just ego. It was craving. A weight on a scale that demanded an equal weight on the other side to balance it out.

The porter returned, poured their wine, and they both sipped. When they were alone again, Mikolas said, "You were right. Grigor wants you."

Viveka paled beneath her already stiff expression. "And you want the merger."

"My grandfather does. I have promised to complete it for him."

She bit her bottom lip so mercilessly it disappeared. "Why?" she demanded. "I mean, why is this merger so important to him?"

"Why does it matter?" he countered.

"Well, what is it you're really trying to accomplish? Surely there are other companies that could give you what you want. Why does it have to be Grigor's?"

She might be impulsive and a complete pain in the backside, but she was perceptive. It *didn't* have to be Grigor's company. He was fully aware of that. However.

"Finding another suitable company would take time we don't have."

"A man with your riches can't buy as much as he needs?" she asked with an ingenuous blink.

She was a like a baby who insisted on trying to catch the tiger's tail and stuff it in her mouth. Not stupid, but cheerfully ignorant of the true danger she was in. He couldn't afford to be lenient.

"My grandfather is ill. I had to call him to tell him the merger has been delayed. That was disappointment he didn't need."

She almost threw an askance look at him, but seemed to read his expression and sobered, getting the message that beneath his civilized exterior lurked a heartless mercenary.

Not that he enjoyed scaring her. He usually treated women like delicate flowers. After sleeping in cold alleys that stank of urine, after being tortured at the hands of degenerate, pitiless men, he'd developed an insatiable appetite for luxury and warmth and the sweet side of life. He especially enjoyed soft kittens who liked to be stroked until they purred next to him in bed.

But if a woman dared to cross him, as with any

man, he ensured she understood her mistake and would never dream of doing so again.

"I owe my grandfather a great deal." He waved at their surroundings. "This."

"I presumed it was stolen," she said with a haughty toss of her head.

"No." He was as blunt as a mallet. "The money was made from smuggling profits, but the boat was purchased legally."

She snapped her head around.

He shrugged, not apologizing for what he came from. "For decades, if something crossed the border or the seas for a thousand miles, legal or illegal, my grandfather—and my father when he was alive— received a cut."

He had her attention. She wasn't saucy now. She was wary. Wondering why he was telling her this.

"Desperate men do desperate things. I know this because I was quite desperate when I began trading on my father's name to survive the streets of Athens."

Their chilled soup arrived. He was hungry, but neither of them moved to pick up their spoons.

"Why were you on the streets?"

"My mother died. Heart failure, or so I was told. I was sent to an orphanage. I hated it." It had been a palace, in retrospect, but he didn't think about that. "I ran away. My mother had told me my father's name. I knew what he was reputed to be. The way my mother had talked, as if his enemies would hunt me down and use me against him if they found me... I thought she was trying to scare me into staying out of trouble.

I didn't," he confided drily. "Boys of twelve are not known for their good judgment."

He smoothed his eyebrow where a scar was barely visible, but he could still feel where the tip of a blade had dragged very deliberately across it, opening the skin while a threat of worse—losing his eye—was voiced.

"I watched and learned from other street gangs and mostly stuck to robbing criminals because they don't go to the police. As long as I was faster and smarter, I survived. Threatening my father's wrath worked well in the beginning, but without a television or computer, I missed the news that he had been stabbed. I was caught in my lie."

Her eyes widened. "What happened?"

"As my mother had warned me, my father's enemies showed great interest. They asked me for information I didn't have."

"What do you mean?" she whispered, gaze fixed to his so tightly all he could see was blue. "Like...?"

"Torture. Yes. My father was known to have stock-piled everything from electronics to drugs to cash. But if I had known where any of it was kept, I would have helped myself, wouldn't I? Rather than trying to steal from them? They took their time believing that." He pretended the recollection didn't coat him in cold sweat.

"Oh, my God." She sat back, fingertips covering her faint words, gaze flickering over her shoulder to where his left hand was still behind her.

Ah. She'd noticed his fingernail.

He brought his hand between them, flexed its stiffness into a fist, then splayed it.

"These two fingernails." He pointed, affecting their removal as casual news. "Several bones broken, but it works well enough after several surgeries. I'm naturally left-handed so that was a nuisance, but I'm quite capable with both now, so…"

"Silver lining?" she huffed, voice strained with disbelief. "How did you get away?"

"They weren't getting anywhere with questioning me and hit upon the idea of asking my grandfather to pay a ransom. He had no knowledge of a grandson, though. He was slow to act. He was grieving. Not pleased to have some pile of dung attempting to benefit off his son's name. I had no proof of my claim. My mother was one of many for my father. That was why she left him."

He shrugged. Female companionship had never been a problem for any of the Petrides men. They were good-looking and powerful and money was seductive. Women found *them*.

"Pappoús could have done many things, not least of which was let them finish killing me. He asked for blood tests before he paid the ransom. When I proved to be his son's bastard, he made me his heir. I suddenly had a clean, dry bed, ample food." He nodded at the beautiful concoction before them: a shallow chowder of corn and buttermilk topped with fat, pink prawns and chopped herbs. "I had anything I wanted. A motorcycle in summer, ski trips in winter. Clothes that were tailored to fit my body in any style or color I asked. Gadgets. A yacht. Anything."

He'd also received a disparate education, tutored by his grandfather's accountant in finance. His real estate and investment licenses were more purchased than earned, but he had eventually mastered the skills to benefit from such transactions. Along the way he had developed a talent for managing people, learning by observing his grandfather's methods. Nowadays they had fully qualified, authentically trained staff to handle every matter. Arm-twisting, even the emotional kind he was utilizing right now, was a retired tactic.

But it was useful in this instance. Viveka needed to understand the bigger picture.

Like his grandfather, he needed a test.

"In return for his generosity, I have dedicated myself to ensuring my grandfather's empire operates on the right side of the law. We're mostly there. This merger is a final step. I have committed to making it happen before his health fails him. You can see why I feel I owe him this."

"Why are you being so frank with me?" Her brow crinkled. "Aren't you afraid I'll repeat any of this?"

"No." Much of it was online, if only as legend and conjecture. While Mikolas had pulled many dodgy stunts like mergers that resembled money laundering, he'd never committed actual crimes.

That wasn't why he was so confident, however.

He held her gaze and waited, watching comprehension solidify as she read his expression. She would not betray him, he telegraphed. Ever.

Her lashes quivered and he watched her swallow.

Fear was beginning to take hold in her. He told himself that was good and ignored the churn of self-contempt in his belly. He wasn't like the men who had tormented him.

But he wasn't that different. Not when he casually picked up his wineglass and mentioned, "I should tell you. Grigor is looking for your sister. You could save yourself by telling him where to find her."

"No!" The word was torn out of her, the look on her face deeply anxious, but not conflicted. "Maybe he never hit her before, but it doesn't mean he wouldn't start now. And this?" She waved at the table and yacht. "She had these trappings all her life and would have given up all of it for a kind word. At least I had memories of our mother. She didn't even have me, thanks to him. So no. *I* would rather go back to Grigor than sell her out to him."

She spoke with brave vehemence, but her eyes grew wet. It wasn't bravado. It was loyalty that would cost her, but she was willing to pay the price.

"I believe you," he pressed with quiet lack of mercy. "That Grigor would resort to violence. The way he spoke when I returned his call—" Mikolas considered himself immune to rabid foaming at the mouth. He knew firsthand how depraved a man could act, but the bloodlust in Grigor's voice had been disturbing. Familiar in a grim, dark way.

And educational. Grigor wasn't upset that his

daughter was missing. He was upset the merger had been delayed. He was taking Viveka's involvement very personally and despite all his posturing and hard-nosed negotiating in the lead-up, he was revealing impatience for the merger to complete.

That told Mikolas his very thorough research prior to starting down this road with Grigor may have missed something. It wasn't a complete surprise that Grigor had kept something up his sleeve. Mikolas had chosen Grigor because he hadn't been fastidious about partnering with the Petrides name. Perhaps Grigor had thought the sacrifice to his reputation meant he could withhold certain debts or other liabilities.

It could turn out that Viveka had done Mikolas a favor, giving him this opportunity to review everything one final time before closing. He could, in fact, gain more than he'd lost.

Either way, Grigor's determination to reach new terms and sign quickly put all the power back in Mikolas's court, exactly where he was most comfortable having it.

Now he would establish that same position with Viveka and his world would be set right.

"Even if he finds her, what can he do to her?" she was murmuring, linking her hands together, nail beds white. "She's married to Stephanos. His boss works for a man who owns news outlets. Big ones. Running her to ground would accomplish nothing. No, she's safe." She seemed to be reassuring herself.

"What about you?" He was surprised she wasn't

thinking of herself. "He sounded like he would hunt you down no matter where you tried to hide." It was the dead-honest truth.

Dead.

Honest.

"So you might as well turn me over and save him the trouble? And close your precious deal with the devil?" So much fire and resentment sparked off her it was fascinating.

"This deal *is* important to me. Grigor knows Pappoús is unwell, that I'm reluctant to look for another option. He wants me to hand you over, close the deal and walk away with what I want—which is to give my grandfather what he wants."

"And what I want doesn't matter." She was afraid, he could see it, but she refused to let it overtake her. He had to admire that.

"You got what you wanted," he pointed out. "Your sister is safe from my evil clutches."

"Good," she insisted, but her mouth quivered before she clamped it into a line. One tiny tear leaked out of the corner of her eye.

Poor, steadfast little kitten.

But that depth of loyalty pleased him. She was passing her test.

He reached out to stroke her hair even though it only made her flinch and flash a look of hatred at him.

"Are you enjoying terrorizing me?"

"Please," he scoffed, taking up his glass of wine to swirl and sip, cooling a mouth that was burning with anticipation as he finalized his decision. "I'm treating you like a Fabergé egg."

He ignored the release of tension inside him as what he really wanted moved closer to his grasp.

"Grigor makes an ugly enemy. You understand why I don't want to make him into one of mine," he said.

"Is it starting to grate on your conscience?" she charged. "That he'll beat me to a pulp and throw me into the nearest body of water? I thought you didn't shame."

"I don't. But I need you to see very clearly that the action I'm taking comes at a cost. Which you will repay. I will not be leaving you in Athens, Viveka. You are staying with me."

CHAPTER FIVE

VIVEKA'S VISION GREW grainy and colorless for a moment. She thought she might pass out, which was not like her at all. She was tough as nails, not given to fainting spells like a Victorian maiden.

She had been subtly hyperventilating this whole time Mikolas had been tying his noose around her neck. Now she'd stopped breathing altogether.

Had she heard him right?

He looked like a god, his neat wedding haircut finger-combed to the side, his mouth symmetrical and unwavering after smiting her with his words. His gray eyes were impassive. Just the facts.

"But—" she started to argue, wanting to bring up Aunt Hildy.

He shook his head. "We're not bargaining. Actions have consequences. These are yours."

"You," she choked, trying to grasp what he was saying. "*You* are my consequence?"

"It's me or Grigor. I've already told you that I won't allow you to hurt yourself, so yes. I have chosen your consequence. We should eat. Before it gets warm," he said with a whimsical levity that struck her as bizarre in the middle of this intense, life-altering conversation.

He picked up his spoon, but she only stared at him. Her fingers were icicles, stiff and frozen. All of her muscles had atrophied while her heart was racing. Her mind stumbled around in the last glimmers of the bleeding sun.

"I have a life in London," she managed. "Things to do."

"I'm sure Grigor knows that and has men waiting."

Her panicked mind sprang to Aunt Hildy, but she was out of harm's reach for the moment. Still, "Mikolas—"

"Think, Viveka. Think hard."

She was trying to. She had been searching for alternatives this whole time.

"So you're abandoning the merger?" She hated the way her voice became puny and confused.

"Not at all. But the terms have changed." He was making short work of his soup and waved his spoon. "With your sister as my wife, Grigor would have had considerable influence over me and our combined organization. I was prepared to let him control his side for up to five years and pay him handsomely for his trouble. Now the takeover becomes hostile and I will push him out, take control of everything and leave him very little. I expect he'll be even more angry with you."

"Then don't be so ruthless! Why aggravate him further?"

His answer was a gentle nudge of his bent knuckle under her chin, thumb brushing the tender place at the corner of her mouth.

"He left a mark on my mistress. He needs to be punished."

Her heart stopped. She jerked back. "Mistress!"

"You thought I was keeping you out of the goodness of my heart?"

Her vision did that wobble again, fading in and out. "You said you didn't want sex." Her voice sounded like it was coming from far away.

"I said I would decide if and when I gave it to you. I have decided. Are you not going to eat those?" He had switched to his fork to eat his prawns and now stabbed one from her bowl, hungrily snapping it between his teeth, but his gaze was watchful when it swung up to hers.

"I'm not having sex with you!"

"You've changed your mind?"

"*You* did," she pointed out tartly, wishing she was one of those women who could be casual about sex. She'd been anxious from the get-go, which was probably why it had turned into this massive issue for her. "I'm not something you can buy like a luxury boat with your ill-gotten gains," she pointed out.

"I haven't purchased you." He gave her a frown of insult. "I've earned your loyalty the same way my grandfather earned mine, by saving your life. You will show your gratitude by being whatever I need you to be, wherever I need you to be."

"I'm not going to be *that*! If I understand you correctly, you want to live within the law. Well, pro tip, forcing women to have sex is against the law."

"Sex will be a fringe benefit for both of us." He was flinty in the face of her sarcasm. "I won't force you and I won't have to."

"Keep. *Dreaming*," she declared.

His fork clattered into his empty bowl and he shifted to face her, one arm behind her, one on the table, bracketing her into a space that enveloped her in masculine energy.

She could have skittered out the far side of the bench, but she held her ground, trying to stare him down.

His gaze fell to her mouth, causing her abdominals to tighten and tremble.

"You're not thinking about it? Wondering? *Dreaming*," he mocked in a voice that jarred because he did *not* sound angry. He sounded amused and knowing. "Let's see, shall we?"

His hand shifted to cup her neck. The caress of his thumb into the hollow at the base of her throat unnerved her. If he'd been forceful, she would have reacted with a slap, but this felt almost tender. She trusted this hand. It had dragged her up to the surface of the water, giving her life.

So she didn't knock that hand away. She didn't hit him in the face as he neared, or pull away to say a hard *No.*

Somehow she got it into her head she would prove he didn't affect her. Maybe she even thought she could return to him that rejection he'd delivered earlier.

Maybe she really did want to know how it would be with him.

Whatever the perverse impulse that possessed her, she sat there and let him draw closer, keeping her mouth set and her gaze as contemptuous as she could make it.

Until his lips touched hers.

If she had expected brutality, she was disappointed. But he wasn't gentle, either.

His hold firmed on her neck as he plundered without hesitation, opening his mouth over hers in a hot, wet branding that caused a burn to explode within her. His tongue stabbed and her lips parted. Delicious swirls of pleasure invaded her belly and lower. Her eyes fluttered closed so she could fully absorb the sensations.

She *had* wondered. Intrigue had held her still for this kiss and she moaned as she basked in it, bones dissolving, muscles weakening.

He kissed her harder, dismantling her attempt to remain detached in a few short, racing heartbeats. He dragged his lips across hers in an erotic crush, the rough-soft texture of his lips like silken velvet.

All her senses came alive to the heat of his chest, the woodsy spice scent on his skin, the salt flavor on his tongue. Her skin grew so sensitized it was painful. She felt vulnerable with longing.

She splayed her free hand against his chest and released a sob of capitulation, no longer just accepting. Participating. Exploring the texture of his tongue, trying to compete with his aggression and consume him with equal fervor.

He pulled back abruptly, the loss of his kiss a cruelty that left her dangling in midair, naked and exposed. His chest moved with harsh breaths that seemed triumphant. The glitter in his eye was superior, asserting that *he* would decide *if* and *when*.

"No force necessary," he said with satisfaction deepening the corners of his mouth.

This was how it had been for her mother, Viveka realized with a crash back to reality. Twenty years ago, Grigor had been handsome and virile, provoking infatuation in a lonely widow. Viveka's earliest memories of being in his house had been ones of walking in on intimate clinches, quickly told to make herself scarce.

As Viveka had matured, she had recognized a similar yearning in herself for a man's loving attention. She understood how desire had been the first means that Grigor had used to control his wife, before encumbering her with a second child, then ultimately showing his ugliest colors to keep her in line.

Sex was a dangerous force that could push a woman down a slippery slope. That was what Viveka had come to believe.

It was doubly perilous when the man in question was so clearly not impacted by their kiss the way she was. Mikolas's indifference hurt, inflicting a loneliness on her that matched those moments in her life that had nearly broken her: losing her mother, being banished from her sister to an aunt who should have loved her, but hadn't.

She had to look away to hide her anguish.

The porter arrived to bring out the next course.

Mikolas didn't even look up from his plate as he said, "What is the name of the man who has your things? I would like to retrieve your passport before Grigor realizes it's under his nose."

Viveka needed to tell him about Aunt Hildy, but didn't trust her voice.

Mikolas said little else through the rest of their meal, only admonishing her to eat, stating at the end of it, "I want to finish the takeover arrangements. You have free run of the yacht unless you show me you need to be confined to your room."

"You seriously think I'll let you keep me like some kind of pirate's doxy?"

"Since I'm about to stage a raid and appoint myself admiral of Grigor's corporate fleet, I can't deny that label, can I? You call yourself whatever you want."

She glared at his back as he walked away.

He left her to her own devices and there must have been something wrong with her because, despite hating Mikolas for his overabundance of confidence, she was viciously glad he was running Grigor through.

At no point should she consider Mikolas her hero, she cautioned herself. She should have known there'd be a cost to his saving her life. She flashed back to Grigor calling her useless baggage. To Hildy telling her to earn her keep.

She wasn't even finished repaying Hildy! That

hardly put her in a position to show "gratitude" to Mikolas, did it?

Oh, she hated when people thought of her as some sort of nuisance. This was why she had been looking forward to settling Hildy and striking out on her own. She could finally prove to herself and the world that she carried her own weight. She was not a lodestone. She wasn't.

A rabbit hole of self-pity beckoned. She avoided it by getting her bearings aboard the aptly named *Inferno*. The top deck was chilly and dark, the early night sky spitting rain into her face as the wind came up. The hot tub looked appealing, steaming and glowing with colored underwater lights. When the porter appeared with towels and a robe, inviting her to use the nearby change room, she was tempted, but explained she was just looking around.

He proceeded to give her a guided tour through the rest of the ship. She didn't know what the official definition for "ship" was, but this behemoth had to qualify. The upper deck held the bridge along with an outdoor bar and lounge at the stern. A spiral staircase in the middle took them down to the interior of the main deck. Along with Mikolas's stateroom and her own, there was a formal dining room for twelve, an elegant lounge with a big-screen television and a baby grand piano. Outside, there was a small lifeboat in the bow, in front of Mikolas's private sundeck, and a huge sunbathing area alongside a pool in the stern.

The extravagance should have filled her with contempt, but instead she was calmed by it, able to pretend this wasn't a boat. It was a seaside hotel. One that happened to be priced well beyond her reach, but *whatever*.

It wasn't as easy to pretend on the lower deck, which was mostly galley, engine room, less extravagant guest and crew quarters. And, oh, yes, another boat, this one a sexy speedboat parked in an internal compartment of the stern.

Her long journey to get to Trina caught up to her at that point. She'd left London the night before and hadn't slept much while traveling. She went back to her suite and changed into a comfortable pair of pajamas—ridiculously pretty ones in peacock-blue silk. Champagne-colored lace edged the bodice and tickled the tops of her bare feet, adding to the feeling of luxuriating in pure femininity.

She hadn't won a prize holiday, she reminded herself, trying not to be affected by all this lavish comfort. A gilded cage was still a prison and she would *not* succumb to Mikolas's blithe expectation that he could "keep" her. He certainly would not *seduce* her with his riches and pampering.

I won't force you and I won't have to.

She flushed anew, recalling their kiss as she curled up on the end of the love seat rather than crawl into bed. She wanted to be awake if he arrived expecting sex. When it came to making love, she was more about fantasy than reality, going only so far with the few men she'd dated. That kiss with Mikolas had shaken her as much as everything else that had happened today.

Better to think about that than her near-drowning, though.

Her thoughts turned for the millionth time to her mother's last moments. Somehow she began imagining her mother was on this boat and they were being tossed about in a storm, but she couldn't find her mother to warn her. It was a dream, she knew it was a dream. She hadn't been on the other boat when her mother was lost, but she could feel the way the waves were battering this one—

Sitting up with a gasp, she sensed they'd hit rough waters. Waves splashed against the glass of her porthole and the boat rocked enough she was rolling on her bed.

How had she wound up in bed?

With a little sob, she threw off the covers and pushed to her feet.

Fear, Aunt Hildy would have said, was no excuse for panic. Viveka did not consider herself a brave person at all, but she had learned to look out for herself because no one else ever had. If this boat was about to capsize, she needed to be on deck wearing a life jacket to have a fighting chance at survival.

Holding the bulkhead as she went into the passageway, she stumbled to the main lounge. The lifeboat was on this deck, she recalled, but in the bow, on the far side of Mikolas's suite. The porter had explained all the safety precautions, which had reassured her at the time. Now all she could think was that it was a stupid place to store life jackets.

Mikolas always slept lightly, but tonight he was on guard for more than old nightmares. He was expecting exactly what happened. The balcony in Viveka's stateroom wasn't the only thing alarmed. When she left her suite, the much more discreet internal security system caused his phone to vibrate.

He acknowledged the signal, then pushed to his feet and adjusted his shorts. That was another reason he'd been restless. He was hard. And he never wore clothes to bed. They were uncomfortable even when they weren't twisted around his erection, but he'd anticipated rising at some point to deal with his guest so he had supposed he should wear something to bed.

He'd expected to find release *with* his guest, but when he'd gone to her room, she'd been fast asleep, curled up on the love seat like a child resisting bedtime, one hand pillowing her cheek. She hadn't stirred when he'd carried her to the bed and tucked her in, leaving him sorely disappointed.

That obvious exhaustion, along with her pale skin and the slight frown between her brows, had plucked a bizarre reaction from him. Something like concern. That bothered him. He was impervious to emotional manipulations, but Viveka was under his skin—and she hadn't even been awake and doing it deliberately.

He sighed with annoyance, moving into his office.

If a woman was going to wake him in the night, it ought to be for better reasons than this.

He had no doubt this private deck in the bow was her destination. He'd watched her talk to his porter extensively about the lifeboat and winch system while he'd sat here working earlier. He wasn't surprised she was attempting to escape. He wasn't even angry. He was disappointed. He hated repeating himself.

But there was an obdurate part of him that enjoyed how she challenged him. Hardly anyone stood up to him anymore.

Plus he was sexually frustrated enough to be pleased she was setting up a midnight confrontation. When he'd kissed her earlier, desire had clawed at his control with such savagery, he'd nearly abandoned one for the other and made love to her right there at the table.

His need to be in command of himself and everyone else had won out in the end. He'd pulled back from the brink, but it had taken more effort than he liked to admit.

"Come on," he muttered, searching for her in the dim glow thrown by the running lights.

This was an addict's reaction, he thought with self-contempt. His brain knew she was lethal, but the way she infused him with a sense of omnipotence was a greater lure. He didn't care that he risked self-destruction. He still wanted her. He was counting the pulse beats until he could feel the rush of her hitting his system.

Where *was* she?

Not overboard again, surely.

The thought sent a disturbing punch into the middle of his chest. He didn't know what had made him throw off his jacket and shoes and dive in after her today. It had been pure instinct. He'd shot out the emergency exit behind her, determined to hear why she had upended his plans, but he hadn't been close enough to stop her tumble into the water.

His heart had jammed when he'd seen her knock into the side of the yacht, worried she was unconscious as she went under.

Pulling her and that whale of a gown to the surface had nearly been more than he could manage. He didn't know what he would have done if the strength of survival hadn't imbued him. Letting go of her hadn't been an option. It wasn't basic human decency that had made him dive into that water, but something far more powerful that refused, absolutely refused, to go back to the surface without her.

Damn it, now he couldn't get that image of her disappearing into the water out of his head. He pushed from his office onto his private deck, where the rain and splashing waves peppered his skin. She wasn't coming down the stairs toward him.

He climbed them, walking along the outer rail of the mid-deck, seeing no sign of her.

Actually, he walked right past her. He spied her when he paused at the door into the bridge, thinking to enter and look for her on the security cameras. Something made him glance back the way he'd come and he spotted the ball of dark clothing and white skin under the life preserver ring.

What the hell?

"Viveka." He retraced his few steps, planting his bare feet carefully on the wet deck. "What are you doing out here?"

She lifted her face. Her hair was plastered in tendrils around her neck and shoulders. Her chin rattled as she stammered, "I n-n-need a l-l-life v-v-vest."

"You're freezing." *He* was cold. He bent to draw her to her feet, but she stubbornly stayed in a knot of trembling muscle, fingers wrapped firmly around the mount for the ring.

What a confounding woman. With a little more force, he started to peel her fingers open.

The boat listed, testing his balance.

Before he could fully right himself, Viveka cried out and nearly knocked him over, rising to throw her arms around his neck, slapping her soaked pajamas into his front.

He swore at the impact, working to stay on his feet.

"Are we going over?"

"No."

He could hardly breathe, she was clinging so tightly to his neck, and shaking so badly he could practically hear her bones rattling. He swore under his breath, putting together all those anxious looks out to the water. This was why she hadn't shown the sense to be terrified of *him* today. She was afraid of boats.

"Come inside." He drew her toward the stairs down to his deck.

She balked. "I don't want to be trapped if we capsize."

"We won't capsize."

She resisted so he picked her up and carried her all the way through his dark office into his stateroom, where he'd left a lamp burning, kicking doors shut along the way.

He sat on the edge of his bed, settling her icy, trembling weight on his lap. "This is only a bit of wind and freighter traffic. We're hitting their wakes. It's not a storm."

There was no heat beneath these soaked pajamas. Even in the dim light, he could see her lips were blue. He ran his hands over her, trying to slick the water out of her pajamas while he rubbed warmth into her skin.

"There doesn't have to be a storm." She was pressing into him, her lips icy against his collarbone, arms still around his neck, relaxing and convulsing in turns. "My mother drowned when it was calm."

"From a boat?" he guessed.

"Grigor took her out." Her voice fractured. "Maybe on purpose to drown her. I don't know, but I think she wanted to leave him. He took her out sailing and said he didn't know till morning that she fell, but he never acted like he cared. He told me to stop crying and take care of Trina."

If this was a trick, it was seriously good acting. The emotion in her voice sent him tumbling into equally disturbing memories buried deep in his subconscious. *Your mother died while you were at school.* The landlord had made the statement without hesitation or regret, casually destroying Mikolas's world with a few simple words. *A woman from child services is coming to get you.*

So much horror had followed, Mikolas barely registered anymore how bad that day had been. He'd shuffled it all into the past once his grandfather had taken him in. The page had been turned and he never leafed back to it.

But suddenly he was stricken with that old grief. He couldn't ignore the way her heart pounded so hard he felt it against his arm across her back. Her skin was clammy, her spine curled tight against life's blows.

His hand unconsciously followed that hard curve, no longer just warming her, but trying to soothe while stealing a long-overdue shred of comfort for himself from someone who understood what he'd suffered.

He recovered just as quickly, shaking off the moment of empathy and rearranging her so she was forced to look up at him.

"I've been honest with you, haven't I?" Perhaps he sounded harsh, but she had cracked something in him. He didn't like the cold wind blowing through him as a result. "I would tell you if we were in danger. We're not."

Viveka believed him. That was the ridiculous part of it. She had no reason to trust him, but why would he be so blunt about everything else and hide the fact they were likely to capsize? If he said they were safe, they were safe.

"I'm still scared," she admitted in a whisper, hating that she was so gutless.

"Think of something else," he chided. The edge of his thumb gave her jaw a little flick, then he dipped his head and kissed her.

She brought up a hand to the side of his face, thinking she shouldn't let this happen again, but his stubble was a fascinating texture against her palm and his lips were blessedly hot, sending runnels of heat through her sluggish blood. Everything in her calmed and warmed.

Then he rocked his mouth to part her lips with the same avid, possessive enjoyment as earlier and cupped her breast and she shuddered under a fresh onslaught of sensations. The rush hurt, it was so powerful, but it was also like that moment when he'd dragged her to the surface. He was dragging her out of her phobia into wonder.

She instinctively angled herself closer, the silk of her pajamas a wet, annoying layer between them as she tried to press herself through his skin.

He grunted and grew harder under her bottom. His arms gathered her in with a confident, sexual possessiveness while his knees splayed wider so she sat deeper against the firm shape of his sex.

Heat rushed into her loins, sharp and powerful. All of her skin burned as blood returned to every inch of her. She didn't mean to let her tongue sweep against his, but his was right there, licking past her lips, and the contact made lightning flash in her belly.

His aggression should have felt threatening, but it

felt sexy and flagrant. As the kiss went on, the waves of pleasure became more focused. The way he toyed with her nipple sent thrums of excitement rocking through her.

She gasped for air when he drew back, but she didn't want to stop. Not yet. She lifted her mouth so he returned and kissed her harder. Deeper.

Her breast ached where he massaged it and the pulse between her legs became a hungry throb as he shifted wet silk against the tight point of her nipple.

His hand slid away, pulling the soggy material up from her quivery belly. He flattened his palm there, branding her cold, bare skin. His fingers searched along the edge of her waistband and he lifted his head, ready to slide his hand between her closed thighs.

"Open," he commanded.

Viveka gasped and shot off his lap, stumbling when her knees didn't want to support her. "What—no!"

She covered her throat where her pulse was racing, shocked at herself. He kept turning her into this… *animal*. That's all this was: hormones. Some kind of primal response to the caveman who happened to yank her out of the lion's jaws. The primitive part of her recognized an alpha male who could keep her offspring alive so her body wanted to make some with him.

Mikolas dropped one hand, then the other behind him, leaning on his straight arms, knees wide. His nostrils flared as he eyed her. It was the only sign that her recoil bothered him.

Contractions of desire continued to swirl in her abdomen. That part of her that was supposed to be able to take his shape felt so achy with carnal need she was nearly overwhelmed.

"You said you wouldn't make me," she managed in a shaky little voice.

It was a weak defense and they both knew it.

He cocked one brow in a mocking, *I don't have to.* The way his gaze traveled down her made her afraid for what she looked like, silk clinging to distended nipples and who knew what other telltale reactions.

She pulled the fabric away from her skin and looked to the door.

"You're bothered by your reaction to me. Why? I think it's exciting." The rasp of his arousal-husky voice made her inner muscles pinch with involuntary eagerness. "Come here. I'll hold you all night. You'll feel very safe," he promised, but his mouth quirked with wicked amusement.

She hugged herself. "I don't sleep around. I don't even know you!"

"I prefer it that way," he provided.

"Well, I don't!"

He sighed, rising and making her heart soar with alarmed excitement. It fell as he turned and walked away to the corner of the room.

She had rejected *him*, she reminded herself. This sense of rebuff was completely misplaced.

But he was so appealing with his tall, powerful frame, spine bracketed by supple muscle in the way of a martial artist rather than a gym junkie. The low light turned his skin a dark, burnished bronze and he had a really nice butt in those wet, clinging boxers.

She ought to leave, but she watched him search out three different points before he drew the wall inward like an oversize door. The cabinetry from her stateroom came with it, folding back to become part of his sitting room, creating an archway into her suite.

"I haven't used this yet. It's clever, isn't it?" he remarked.

If she didn't loathe boats so much, she might have agreed. As it was, she could only hug herself, dumbfounded to see they were now sharing a room.

"You'll feel safer like this, yes?"

Not likely!

He didn't seem to expect an answer, just turned to open a drawer. He pawed through, coming up with a pink long-sleeved top in waffle weave and a pair of pink and mint green flannel pajama pants. "Dry off and put these on. Warm up."

She waved at the archway. "Why did you do that?"

"You don't find it comforting?"

Oh, she was not sticking around to be laughed at. She snatched the pajamas from his hand, not daring to look into his face, certain she would see mockery, and made for the bathroom in her own suite. *Infuriating* man.

She would close the wall herself, she decided as she clumsily changed, even though she preferred the idea of him being in the same room with her. He was not a man to be relied on, she reminded herself. If she had learned nothing else in life, it was that she was on her own.

Then she walked out and found a life vest on the foot of her bed. When she glanced toward his room, his lamp was off.

She clutched the cool bulk of the vest to her chest, insides crumpling.

"Thank you, Mikolas," she said toward his darkened room.

A pause, then a weary "Try not to need it."

CHAPTER SIX

Viveka was so emotionally spent, she slept late, waking with the life vest still in her crooked arm.

Sitting up with an abrupt return of memory, she noted the sun was streaming in through the uncovered windows of Mikolas's stateroom. The yacht was sailing smoothly and she could swear that was the fresh scent of a light breeze she detected. She swung her feet to the floor and moved into his suite with a blink at the brightness.

He didn't notice her, but she caught her breath at the sight of him. He was lounging on the wing-like extension from his sitting area. It was fronted by what looked like the bulkhead of his suite and fenced on either side by glass panels anchored into thin, stainless steel uprights. The wind blew over him, ruffling his dark hair.

She might have been alarmed by the way the ledge dangled over the water, but he was so relaxed, slouched on a cushioned chair, feet on an ottoman, she could only experience again the pinch of deep attraction.

He had his tablet in one hand, a half-eaten apple

in the other and he was mostly naked. Again. All he wore were shorts, these ones a casual pair in checked gray and black even though the morning breeze was quite cool.

Her heart actually panged that she had to keep fighting him. He looked so casually beautiful. It wasn't just about her, though, but Aunt Hildy.

He lifted his head and turned to look at her as though he'd been aware of her the whole time. "Are you afraid to come out here?"

She was terrified, but it had nothing to do with the water and everything to do with how he affected her.

"Why are you allowed to have your balcony open and I got in trouble for it?" she asked, choosing a tone of belligerence over revealing her intimidation, forcing her legs to carry her as far as the opening.

"I had a visitor." He nodded at the deck beside his ottoman.

Her bag.

Stunned, she quickly knelt and rifled through it, coming up with her purse, phone, passport… Everything exactly as it should be. Even her favorite hair clip. She gathered and rolled the mess of her hair in a well-practiced move, weirdly comforted by that tiny shred of normalcy.

When she looked up at him, Mikolas was watching her. He finished his apple with a couple of healthy bites and flipped the core into the water.

"Help yourself." He nodded toward where a sideboard was set up next to the door to his office.

"I'm in time-out? Not allowed out for breakfast?"

No response, but she quickly saw there was more than coffee and a basket of fruit here. The dishes contained traditional favorites she hadn't eaten since leaving Greece nine years ago.

Somehow she'd convinced herself she hated everything about this country, but the moment she saw the *tiganites*, nostalgia closed her throat. A sharp memory of asking her mother if she could cut up her sister's pancakes and pour the *petimezi* came to her. Nothing tasted quite like grape molasses. Her heart panged, while her mouth watered and her stomach contracted with hunger.

"Have you eaten?" she called, hoping he didn't hear the break in her voice. She glanced out to see he didn't have a plate going.

"Óchi akóma." Not yet.

She gave him a large helping of the smoked pork omelet along with pancakes and topped up his coffee, earning a considering look as she served him.

Yes, she was trying to soften him up. A woman had to create advantages where she could with a man like him.

"Efcharistó," he said when she joined him.

"Parakaló." She was trying to act casual, but she had chosen to start with yogurt and thyme honey. The first bite tasted so perfect, was such a burst of early childhood happiness, when her mother had been alive and her sister a living doll she could dress and feed, she had to close her eyes, pressing back tears of homecoming.

* * *

Mikolas watched her, reluctantly fascinated by the emotion that drew her cheeks in while she savored her breakfast. Pained joy crinkled her brow. It was sensual and sexy and poignant. It was *yogurt*.

He forced his gaze to his own plate.

Viveka was occupying entirely too much real estate in his brain. It had to stop.

But even as he told himself that, his mind went back to last night. How could it not, with her sitting across from him braless beneath her long-sleeved nightshirt? The soft weight of her breast was still imprinted on his palm, firm and shapely, topped with a sensitive nipple he'd longed to suck.

Instantly he was primed for sex. And damn it, she'd been as fully involved as he had been. He wasn't so arrogant he made assumptions about women's states of interest. He took pains to ensure they were with him every step of the way when he made love to them. She'd been pressing herself into him, returning his kiss, moaning with enjoyment.

Fine, he could accept that she thought they were moving too fast. Obviously she was a bit of a romantic, flying across the continent to help her sister marry her first love. But sex would happen between them. It was inevitable.

When he had opened the passageway between their rooms, however, it hadn't been for sex. He had wanted to ease her anxiety. She had been nothing less than a nuclear bomb from the moment he'd seen her face, but he'd found himself searching out the catch in the wall, giving her access to *his* space, which had never been his habit with any woman.

He didn't understand his actions around her. This morning, he'd actually begun second-guessing his decision to keep her, which wasn't like him at all. Indecision did not make for control in any situation. He certainly couldn't back down because he was *scared*. Of being around a particular *woman*.

Then the news had come through that Grigor was, indeed, hiding debts in two of his subsidiaries. There was no room for equivocating after that. Mikolas had issued a few terse final orders, then notified Grigor of his intention to take over with or without cooperation.

Grigor had been livid.

Given the man's vile remarks, Mikolas was now as suspicious as Viveka that her stepfather had killed her mother. Viveka would stay with him whether he was comfortable in her presence or not.

Whether she liked it or not. At least until he could be sure Grigor wouldn't harm her.

She opened her dreamy blue eyes and looked like she was coming back from orgasm. Sexual awareness shimmered like waves of desert heat between them.

Yes. Sex was inevitable.

Her gaze began to tangle with his, but she seemed to take herself in hand. She sat taller and cleared her throat, looking out to the water and lifting a determined chin, cheekbones glowing with pink heat.

He mentally sighed, too experienced a fighter not to recognize she was preparing to start one.

"Mikolas." He mentally applauded her take-charge tone. "I *have* to go back to London. My aunt is very old. Quite ill. She needs me."

He absorbed that with a blink. This was a fresh approach at least.

She must have read his skepticism. Her mouth tightened. "I wish I was making it up. I'm not."

If he expected her trust—and he did—he would have to trust her in return, he supposed. "Tell me about her," he invited.

She looked to the clear sky, seeming to struggle a moment.

"There's not much to tell. She's the sister of my grandmother and took me in when Grigor kicked me out, even though she was a spinster who never wanted anything to do with children. She had a career before women really did. Worked in Parliament, but not as an elected official. As a secretary to a string of them. She had some kind of lofty clearance, served coffee to all sorts of royals and diplomats. I think she was in love with a married man," she confided with a wrinkle of her nose.

Definitely a sentimentalist.

She shrugged, murmuring, "I don't have proof. Just a few things she said over the years." She picked up her coffee and cupped her hands around it. "She was always telling me how to behave so men wouldn't think things." She made a face. "I'm sure the sexism in her day was appalling. She was adamant that I be independent, pay my share of rent and groceries, know how to look after myself."

"She didn't take her own advice? Make arrangements for herself?"

"She tried." Her shoulder hitched in a helpless shrug. "Like a lot of people, she lost her retirement savings with the economic crash. For a while she had an income bringing in boarders, but we had to stop that a few years ago and remortgage. She has dementia." Her sigh held the weight of the world. "Strangers in the house upset her. She doesn't recognize me anymore, thinks I'm my mother, or her sister, or an intruder who stole her groceries." She looked into her cooling coffee. "I've begun making arrangements to put her into a nursing home, but the plans aren't finalized."

Viveka knew he was listening intently, thought about leaving it there, where she had stopped with the doctors and the intake staff and with Trina during their video chats. But the mass on her conscience was too great. She'd already told Mikolas about Grigor's abuse. He might actually understand the rest and she really needed it off her chest.

"I *feel* like I'm stealing from her. She worked really hard for her home and deserves to live in it, but she can't take care of herself. I have to run home from work every few hours to make sure she hasn't started a fire or caught a bus to who knows where. I can't afford to stay home with her all day and even if I could…"

She swallowed, reminding herself not to feel resentful, but it still hurt. Not just physically, either.

She had tried from Day One to have a familial relationship with her aunt and it had all been for naught.

"She started hitting me. I know she doesn't mean it to be cruel. She's scared. She doesn't understand what's happening to her. But I can't take it."

She couldn't look at him. She already felt like the lowest form of life and he wasn't saying anything. Maybe he was letting her pour out her heart and having a laugh at her for getting smacked by an old lady.

"Living with her was never great. She's always been a difficult, demanding person. I was planning to move out the minute I finished school, but she started to go downhill. I stayed to keep house and make meals and it's come to this."

The little food she'd eaten felt like glue in her stomach. She finished up with the best argument she could muster.

"You said you're loyal to your grandfather for what he gave you. That's how I feel toward her. The only way I can live with removing her from her home is by making sure she goes to a good place. So I have to go back to London and oversee that."

Setting aside her coffee, she hugged herself, staring sightlessly at the horizon, not sure if it was guilt churning her stomach or angst at revealing herself this way.

"Now who is beating you up?" Mikolas challenged.

She swung her head to look at him. "You don't think I owe her? Someone needs to advocate for her."

"Where is she now?"

"I was coming away so I made arrangements with

her doctor for her to go into an extended-care facility. It's just for assessment and referral, though. The formal arrangements have to be completed. She can't stay where she is and she can't go home if I'm not there. Her doctor is expecting me for a consult this week."

Mikolas reached for his tablet and tapped to place a call. A moment later, the tablet chimed. Someone answered in German. They had a lengthy conversation that she didn't understand. Mikolas ended with, *"Dankeschön."*

"Who was that?" she asked as he set aside the tablet.

"My grandfather's doctor. He's Swiss. He has excellent connections with private clinics all over Europe. He'll ensure Hildy is taken into a good one."

She snorted. "Neither of us has the kind of funds that will underwrite a private clinic arranged by a posh specialist from Switzerland. I can barely afford the extra fees for the one I'm hoping will take her."

"I'll do this for you, to put your mind at ease."

Her mind blanked for a full ten seconds.

"Mikolas," she finally sputtered. "I *want* to do it. I definitely don't want to be in your debt over it!" She ignored the fact that he had already decided she owed him.

Men expect things when they do you a favor, she heard Hildy saying.

A lurching sensation yanked at her heart, like a curtain being pulled aside on its rungs, exposing her at her deepest level. "What kind of sex do you think you're going to get out of me that would possibly compensate you for something like that? Because I can assure you, I'm not that good! You'll be disappointed."

So disappointed.

Had she just said "you'll"? Like she was a sure thing?

She tightened her arms across herself, refusing to look at him as this confrontation took the direction she had hoped it wouldn't: right into the red-light district of Sexville.

"If that sounds like I just agreed to have sex with you, that's not what I meant," Viveka bit out, voice less strident, but still filled with ire.

Mikolas couldn't think of another woman he'd encountered with such an easily tortured conscience or with such a valiant determination to protect people she cared about while completely disregarding the cost to herself.

She barely seemed real. He was in danger of being *moved* by her depth of loyalty toward her aunt. A jaded part of him had to question whether she was doing exactly what she claimed she wasn't: trying to manipulate him into underwriting the old woman's care, but unlike most women in his sphere, she wasn't offering sex as compensation for making her problems go away.

While he was finding the idea of her coming to his bed motivated by anything other than the same passion that gripped him more intolerable by the second.

"Let us be clear," he said with abrupt decision. "The debt you owe me is the loss of a wife."

She didn't move, but her blue eyes lifted to fix on him, watchful and limitless as the sky.

"My intention was to marry, honeymoon this week, then throw a reception for my new bride, introducing her to a social circle that has been less than welcoming to someone with my pedigree when I only ever had a mistress du jour on my arm."

Being an outsider didn't bother him. He had conditioned himself not to need approval or acceptance from anyone. He preferred his own company and had his grandfather to talk to if he grew bored with himself.

But ostracism didn't sit well with a nature that demanded to overcome any circumstance. The more he worked at growing the corporation, the more he recognized the importance of networking with the mainstream. Socializing was an annoying way to spend his valuable time, but necessary.

"Curiosity, if nothing else, would have brought people to the party," he continued. "The permanence of my marriage would have set the stage for developing other relationships. You understand? Wives don't form friendships with women they never see again. Husbands don't encourage their wives to invite other men's temporary liaisons for drinks or dinner."

"Because they're afraid their wives will hear about their own liaisons?" she hazarded with an ingenuous blink.

Really, no sense of self-preservation.

"It's a question of investment. No one wants to put time or money into something that lacks a stable future. I was gaining more than Grigor's company by marrying. It was a necessary shift in my image."

Viveka shook her head. "Trina would have been hopeless at what you're talking about. She's sweet and funny, loves to cook and pick flowers for arrangements. You couldn't ask for a kinder ear if you need to vent, but playing the society wife? Making small talk about haute couture and trips to the Maldives? You, with your sledgehammer personality, would have crushed her before she was dressed, let alone an evening trying to find her place in the pecking order of upper-crust hens."

"Sledgehammer," he repeated, then accused facetiously, "Flirt."

She blushed. It was pretty and self-conscious and fueled by this ivory-tusked, sexual awareness they were both pretending to ignore. Her gaze flashed to his, naked and filled with last night's trance-like kiss. Her nipples pricked to life beneath the pink of her shirt. So did the flesh between his legs. The moment became so sexually infused, he almost lost the plot.

That's how he wanted it to be between them: pure reaction. Not installment payments.

He reined himself in with excruciating effort, throat tight and body readied with tension as he continued.

"Circulating with the woman who broke up my wedding is not ideal, but will look better than escorting a rebound after being thrown over. Since you'll be with me until I've neutralized Grigor, we will be able to build that same message of constancy."

"What do you mean about neutralizing Grigor?"

"I spoke to him this morning. He's not pleased with my takeover or the fact you're staying with me. You need some serious protections in place. Did you have your mother's death investigated?"

That seemed to throw her. Her face spasmed with emotion.

"I was only nine when it happened so it was years before I really put it all together and thought he could have done it. I was fourteen when I asked the police to look into it, but they didn't take me seriously. The police on the island are in his pocket. The whole island is and I don't really blame them. I've learned myself that you play by his rules or lose everything. Probably the only reason he didn't kill me for making a statement was because it would have been awfully suspicious if something happened to me right after my complaint. But stirring up questions was one of the reasons he kicked me out. Why?"

"I will hire a private investigator to see what we can find. If something can be proved and he's put in prison, you'll be out of his reach."

"That could take years!"

"And will make him that much more incensed with you in the short term," he said drily. "But as you say, if he's under suspicion, it wouldn't look good if anything happened to you. I think it will afford you protection in the long term."

"You're going to start an investigation, take care

of my aunt and protect me from Grigor and all I have to do is pretend to be your girlfriend." Her voice rang with disbelief. "For how *long*?"

"At least until the merger completes and the investigation shows some results. Play your part well and you might even earn my forgiveness for disrupting my life so thoroughly."

Her laugh was ragged and humorless. "And sex?"

She tossed her head, affecting insouciance, but the small frown between her brows told him she was anxious. That aggravated him. He could think of nothing else but discovering exactly how incendiary they would be together. If she wasn't equally obsessed, he was at a disadvantage.

Not something he ever endured.

With a casual flick of his hand, he proclaimed, "Like today's fine weather, we'll enjoy it because it's there."

Did a little shadow of disappointment pass behind her eyes? What did she expect? Lies about falling in love? They really were at an impasse if she expected that ruse.

Her mouth pursed to disguise what might have been a brief tremble. She pushed to stand. "Yes, well, the almanac is predicting heavy frost. Dress warm." She reached for her bag. "I'm going to my room."

"Leave your passport with me."

She turned back to regard him with what he was starting to think of as her princess look, very haughty and down the nose. "Why?"

"To arrange travel visas."

"To where?"

"Wherever I need you to be."

"Give me a 'for instance.'"

"Asia, eventually, but you wanted to go to Athens, didn't you? There's a party tonight. Do as you're told and I'll let you off the boat to come with me."

Her spine went very straight at that patronizing remark. Her unfettered breasts were not particularly heavy, but magnificent in their shape and firmness and chill-sharpened points. He was going to go out of his mind if he didn't touch her again soon.

As if she read his thoughts, her brows tugged together with conflict. She was no doubt thinking that the return of her purse and arrival in Athens equaled an excellent opportunity to set him in the rearview mirror.

He tensed, waiting out the minutes of her indecision. Oddly, it was not unlike the anticipation of pain. His breath stilled in his lungs, throat tight, as he willed her to do as he said.

Do not make me ask again.

Helplessness flashed in her expression before she ducked her head and drew her passport out of her bag, hand trembling as she held it out to him.

A debilitating rush of relief made his own arm feel like it didn't even belong to him. He reached to take it.

She held on while she held his gaze, incredibly beautiful with that hard-won determination lighting her proud expression. "You *will* make sure Aunt Hildy is properly cared for?"

"You and Pappoús will get along well. He holds me to my promises, too."

She released the passport into his possession, averting her gaze as though she didn't want to acknowledge the significance. Clearing her throat, she took out her phone. "I want to check in with Trina. May I have the WiFi code?"

"The security key is a mix of English and Greek characters." He held out his other hand. "I'll do it for you."

She released a noise of impatient defeat, slapped her phone into his palm and walked away.

CHAPTER SEVEN

Mikolas had set himself up in her contacts with a selfie taken on her phone, of him sitting there like a sultan on his yacht, taking ownership of her entire life.

She couldn't stop looking at it. Those smoky eyes of his were practically making love to her, the curve of his wide mouth quirked at the corners in not quite a smile. It was more like, *I know you're naked in the shower right now.* He was so brutally handsome with his chiseled cheekbones and devil-doesn't-give-a-damn nonchalance he made her chest hurt.

Yet he had also forwarded a request from the Swiss doctor for her aunt's details along with a recommendation for one of those beyond-top-notch dementia villages that were completely unattainable for mere mortals. A quick scan of its website told her it was very patient-centric and prided itself on compassion and being ahead of the curve with quality treatment. All that was needed was the name of her aunt's physician to begin Hildy's transfer into the facility's care.

Along with Trina's well-being, a good plan for

Aunt Hildy was the one thing Viveka would sell her soul for. It was a sad commentary on her life that it was the only thing pulling her back to London. She had no community there, rarely had time for dating or going out with friends. Her neighbor was nice, but mostly her life had revolved around school, then work and caring for Aunt Hildy. There was no one worrying about her now, when she had been stolen like a concubine by this throwback Spartan warrior.

She sighed, not even able to argue that her job was a career she needed to get back to. One quick email and her position had been snapped up by one of the part-timers who need the hours. She'd be on the bottom rung when she went back. If she went back. She'd accepted that job for its convenience to home, and in the back of her mind, she'd already been planning to make a change once she had Hildy settled.

But Aunt Hildy had faced nothing but challenges all her life and, in her way, she'd been Viveka's lifeline. The old woman shouldn't have to suffer and wouldn't. Not if Viveka could help it.

And now that Mikolas had spelled out that sex wasn't mandatory...

Oh, she didn't want to think about sex with that man! He already made her feel so unlike herself she could hardly stand it. But she couldn't help wondering what it would be like to lie with him. Something about him got to her, making her blood run like cavalry into sensual battle. Sadly, Viveka had reservations that made the idea of being intimate with him seem not just ill-advised but completely impossible.

So she tried not to think of it and video-called Trina. Her sister was both deliriously joyful and terribly worried when she picked up.

"Where *are* you? Papa is furious." Her eyes were wide. "I'm scared for you, Vivi."

"I'm okay," she prevaricated. "What about you? You've obviously talked to him. Is he likely to come after you?"

"He doesn't believe this was my decision. He blames you for all of it and it sounds—I'm not sure what's going on at his office, but things are off the rails and he thinks it's your fault. I'm so sorry, Vivi."

"That doesn't surprise me," Viveka snorted, hiding how scared the news made her. "Are you and Stephanos happy? Was all of this worth it?"

"So happy! I knew he was my soul mate, but oh, Vivi!" Her sister blushed, growing even more radiant, saying in a self-conscious near-whisper, "Being married is even better than I imagined it would be."

Lovemaking. That's what her little sister was really talking about.

Envy, acute and painful, seared through Viveka. She had always felt left out when women traded stories about men and intimacy. Dating for her had mostly been disastrous. Now even her younger sister was ahead of her on that curve. It made Viveka even more insecure in her sexuality than she already was.

They talked a few more minutes and Viveka was wistful when she ended the call. She was glad Trina was living happily-ever-after. At one time, she'd believed in that fairy tale for herself, but had become more pragmatic over the years, first by watching the nightmare that her mother's romance turned into, then challenged by Aunt Hildy for wanting a man to "complete" her.

She hadn't thought of it that way, exactly. Finding a soul mate was a stretch, true, but why shouldn't she want a companion in life? What was the alternative? Live alone and lonely, like Aunt Hildy? Engage in casual hookups like Mikolas had said he preferred?

She was not built for fair-weather frolics.

Her introspection was interrupted by a call from Hildy's doctor. He was impressed that she was able to get her aunt into that particular clinic and wanted to make arrangements to move her the next morning. He assured Viveka she was doing the right thing.

The die was cast. Not long after, the ship docked and Viveka and Mikolas were whisked into a helicopter. It deposited them on top of *his* building, which was an office tower, but he had a penthouse that took up most of an upper floor.

"I have meetings this afternoon," he told her. "A stylist will be here shortly to help you get ready."

Viveka was typically ready to go out within thirty minutes. That included shampooing and drying her hair. She had never in her life started four hours before an appointment, not even when she had fake-married the man who calmly left her passport on a side table like bait and walked out.

Not that this world was so different from living with Grigor, Viveka thought, lifting her baleful gaze from the temptation of her passport to gaze around

Mikolas's private domain. Grigor had been a bully, but he'd lived very well. His island mansion had had all the same accoutrements she found in Mikolas's penthouse: a guest room with a full bath, a well-stocked wine fridge and pantry, a pool on a deck overlooking a stunning view.

None of it put her at ease. She was still nervous. Expectation hung over her. Or rather, the question of what Mikolas expected.

And whether she could deliver.

Not sex, she reminded herself, trying to keep her mind off that. She turned to tormenting herself with anxiety over how well she would perform in the social arena. She wasn't shy, but she wasn't particularly out-going. She wasn't particularly pretty, either, and she had a feeling every other woman at this party would be gorgeous if Mikolas thought she needed four hours of beautification to bring her up to par.

The stylist's preparation wasn't all shoring up of her looks, however. It was pampering with massage and a mani-pedi, encouragement to doze by the pool while last-minute adjustments were made to her dress, and a final polish on her hair and makeup that gave her more confidence than she expected.

As she eyed herself in the gold cocktail dress, she was floored at how chic she looked. The cowled hal-ter bodice hung low across her modest chest and the snug fabric hugged her hips in a way that flattered her figure without being obvious. The color brought out the lighter strands in her hair and made her skin look like fresh cream.

The stylist had trimmed her mop, then let its natural wave take over, only parting it to the side and adding two little pins so her face was prettily framed while the rest fell away in a shiny waterfall around her shoulders. She applied false eyelashes, but they were just long enough to make her feel extra feminine, not ridiculous.

"I've never known how to make my bottom lip look as wide as the top," Viveka complained as her lips were painted. The bruise Grigor had left there had faded overnight to unnoticeable.

"Why would you want to?" the woman chided her. "You have a very classic look. Like old Hollywood."

Viveka snorted, but she'd take it.

She had to acknowledge she was delighted with the end result, but became shy when she moved into the lounge to find Mikolas waiting for her.

He took her breath, standing at the window with a drink in his hand. He'd paired his suit with a gray shirt and charcoal tie, ever the dark horse. It was all cut to perfection against his frame. His profile was silhouetted against the glow of the Acropolis in the distance. *Zeus*, she thought, and her knees weakened.

He turned his head and even though he was already quite motionless, she sensed time stopping. Maybe they both held their breath. She certainly did, anxious for kind judgment.

Behind her, the stylist left, leaving more tension as the quiet of the apartment settled with the departure of the lift.

Viveka's eyes dampened. She swallowed to ease

the dryness in the back of her throat. "I have no idea how to act in this situation," she confessed.

"A date?" he drawled, drawing in a breath as though coming back to life.

"Is that all it is?" Why did it feel so monumental? "I keep thinking that I'm supposed to act like we're involved, but I don't know much about you."

"Don't you?" His cheek ticked and she had the impression he didn't like how much she did know.

"I guess I know you're the kind of man who saves a stranger's life."

That seemed to surprise him.

She searched his enigmatic gaze, asking softly, "Why did you?" Her voice held all of the turbulent emotions he had provoked with the act.

"It was nothing," he dismissed, looking away to set down his glass.

"Please don't say that." But was it realistic to think her life had meant something to him after one glimpse? No. Her heart squeezed. "It wasn't nothing to me."

"I don't know," he admitted tightly. His eyes moved over her like he was looking for clues. "But I wasn't thinking ahead to this. Saving a person's life shouldn't be contingent on repayment. I just reacted."

Unlike his grandfather, who had wanted to know he was actually getting his grandson before stepping in. *Oh, Mikolas.*

For a moment, the walls between them were gone and the bright, magnetic thing between them tugged. She wanted to move forward and offer comfort. Be whatever he needed her to be.

For one second, he seemed to hover on a tipping point. Then a layer of aloofness fell over him like a cloak.

"I don't think anyone will have trouble believing we're involved when you look at me like that." He smiled, but it was a tad cruel. "If I wasn't finally catching up to someone I've been chasing for a while, I would accept your invitation. But I have other priorities."

She flinched, stunned by the snub.

Fortunately he didn't see it, having turned away to press the call button to bring back the elevator.

She moved on stiff legs to join him, fighting tears of wounded self-worth. Her throat ached. Compassion wasn't a character flaw, she reminded herself. Just because Grigor and Hildy and this *jackass* weren't capable of appreciating what she offered didn't mean she was worthless.

She couldn't help her reaction to him. Maybe if she wasn't such an incurable *virgin*, she'd be able to handle him, she thought furiously, but that's what she was and she hated him for taunting her with it.

She was wallowing so deep in silent offense, she moved automatically, leaving the elevator as the doors opened, barely taking in her surroundings until she heard her worst nightmare say, *"There she is."*

CHAPTER EIGHT

MIKOLAS WAS KICKING himself as the elevator came to a halt.

Viveka had been so beautiful when she had walked into the lounge, his heart had lurched. An unfamiliar lightheartedness had overcome him. It hadn't been the money spent on her appearance. It was the authentic beauty that shone through all the labels and products, the kind that waterfalls and sunsets possessed. You couldn't buy that kind of awe-inspiring magnificence. You couldn't ignore it, either, when it was right in front of you. And when you let yourself appreciate it, it felt almost healing...

He never engaged in rose smelling and sunset gazing. He lived in an armored tank of wealth, emotional distance and superficial relationships. His dates were formalities, a type of foreplay. It wasn't sexism. He invested even less in his dealings with men.

His circle never included people as unguarded as Viveka, with her defensive shyness and yearning for acceptance. Somehow that guilelessness of hers got through his barriers as aggression never would. She'd asked him why he'd saved her life and before he knew it, he was reliving the memory of pleading with everything in him for his grandfather—a stranger at the time—to save *him*.

Erebus hadn't.

Not right away. Not without proof.

Words such as *despair* and *anguish* were not strong enough to describe what came over him when he thought back to it.

She had had an idea what it was, though, without his having to say a word. He had seen more in her eyes than an offer of sex. Empathy, maybe. Whatever it was, it had been something so real, it had scared the hell out of him. He couldn't lie with a woman when his inner psyche was torn open that far. Who knew what else would spill out?

He needed escape and she needed to stay the hell back.

He was so focused on achieving that, he walked out of the elevator not nearly as aware of his surroundings as he should be.

As they came alongside the security desk, he heard, "There she is," and turned to see Grigor lunging at Viveka, nearly pulling her off her feet, filthy vitriol spewing over her scream of alarm.

"—think you can investigate me? I'll show you what murder looks like—"

Reflex took over and Mikolas had broken Grigor's nose before he knew what he was doing.

Grigor fell to the floor, blood leaking between his clutching fingers. Mikolas bent to grab him by the collar, but his security team rushed in from all directions, pressing Mikolas's Neanderthal brain back into its cave.

"Call the police," he bit out, straightening and putting his arm around Viveka. "Make sure you mention his threats against her life."

He escorted Viveka outside to his waiting limo, afraid, genuinely afraid, of what he would do to the man if he stayed.

As her adrenaline rush faded in the safety of the limo, Viveka went from what felt like a screaming pitch of tension to being a spent match, brittle and thin, charred and cold.

It wasn't just Grigor surprising her like that. It was how crazed he'd seemed. If Mikolas hadn't stepped in... But he had and seeing Grigor on the receiving end of the sickening thud of a fist connecting to flesh wasn't as satisfying as she had always imagined it would be.

She *hated* violence.

She figured Mikolas must feel the same, given his past. Those last minutes as they'd come downstairs kept replaying in her mind. She'd been filled with resentment as they'd left the elevator, hotly thinking that if saving a person's life didn't require repayment, why was he forcing her to go to this stupid party? He said she was under his protection, but it was more like she was under his thumb.

But the minute she was threatened, the very second it had happened, he had leaped in to save her. Again.

It was as ground-shaking as the first time.

Especially when the aftermath had him feeling the bones in his repaired hand like he was checking for fractures. His thick silence made her feel sick.

"Mikolas, I'm sorry," Viveka said in a voice that flaked like dry paint.

She was aware of his head swinging around but couldn't look at him.

"You know I only had Trina's interest at heart when I came to Greece, but it was inconsiderate to you. I didn't appreciate the situation I was putting you in with Grigor—"

"That's enough, Viveka."

She jolted, stung by the graveled tone. It made the blood congeal in her veins and she hunched deeper into her seat, turning her gaze to the window.

"That was my fault." Self-recrimination gave his voice a bitter edge. "We signed papers for the merger today. I made sure he knew why I was squeezing him out. He tried to cheat me."

It was her turn to swing a surprised look at him. He looked like he was barely holding himself in check.

"I wouldn't have discovered it until after I was married to Trina, but your interference gave me a chance to review everything. I wound up getting a lot of concessions beyond our original deal. Things were quite ugly by the end. He was already blaming you so I told him I'd started an investigation. I should have expected something like this. I owe *you* the apology."

She didn't know what to say.

"You helped me by stopping the wedding. Thank you. I hope to hell the investigation puts him in jail," he added tightly.

He was staring at her intently, nostrils flared.

Her mouth trembled. She felt awkward and shy and tried to cover it with a lame attempt at levity. "Between Grigor and Hildy, I've spent most of my life being told I was an albatross of one kind or another. It's refreshing to hear I've had a positive effect for once. I thought for sure you were going to yell at me…" Her voice broke.

She sniffed and tried to catch a tear with a trembling hand before it ruined her makeup.

He swore and before she realized what he was doing, he had her in his lap.

"Did he hurt you? Let me see your arm where he grabbed you," he demanded, his touch incredibly gentle as he lightly explored.

"Don't be sweet to me right now, Mikolas. I'll fall apart."

"You prefer the goon from the lobby?" he growled, making a semihysterical laugh bubble up.

"You're not a goon," she protested, but obeyed the hard arms that closed around her and cuddled into him, numb fingers stealing under the edge of his jacket to warm against his steady heartbeat.

He ran soothing hands over her and let out a breath, tension easing from both of them in small increments.

She was still feeling shaky when they reached the Makricosta Olympus.

"I hate these things," he muttered as he escorted

her to the brightly decorated ballroom. "We should have stayed in."

Too late to leave. People were noting their entrance.

"Do you mind if I…?" she asked as she spotted the ladies' room off to the right. She could only imagine how she looked.

A muscle pulsed in his jaw, like he didn't want her out of his sight, but after one dismayed heartbeat he said, "I'll be at the bar."

Reeling under an onslaught of gratitude and confusion and yearning, she hurried to the powder room and moved directly to the mirror to check her makeup. She felt like a disaster, but had only a couple of smudges to dab away.

"Synchórisi," the woman next to her said, gaze down as she fiddled with the straps on her shimmery black dress. Releasing a distinctly British curse she said, "My Greek is nonexistent. Is there any chance you speak English?"

Viveka straightened from the mirror, taking a breath to gather her composure. "I do."

"Oh, you're upset." The woman was a delicate blonde and her smile turned concerned. "I'm sorry. I shouldn't have bothered you."

"No, I'm fine," she dismissed with a wobbly smile. The woman was doing her a favor, not letting her dwell on all the mixed emotions coursing through her. "Not the bad kind of crying."

"Oh, did he do something nice?" she asked with a pleased grin. "Because husbands really ought to, now and again."

"He's not my husband, but…" Viveka thought of Mikolas saving her and thanking her for the wedding debacle. Her heart wobbled again and she had to swallow back a fresh rush of emotion. "He did."

"Good. I'm Clair, by the way." She offered her free hand to shake while her other hand stayed against her chest, the straps of her halter-style bodice dangling over her slender fingers.

"Viveka. Call me Vivi." Eyeing the straps, she guessed, "Wardrobe malfunction?"

"The worst! Is there any chance you have a pin?"

"I don't. Can you tie them?" She circled her finger in the air. "Turn around. Let's see what happened to the catch."

They quickly determined the catch was long gone and they were too short to tie.

"I bet a tiepin would hold it. Give me a minute. I'll ask Mikolas for his," Viveka offered.

"Good idea, but ask my husband," Clair said. "Then I won't have to worry about returning it."

Viveka chuckled. "Let me guess. Your husband is the man in the suit?" She thumbed toward the ballroom filled with a hundred men wearing ties and jackets.

Clair grinned. "Mine's easy to spot. He's the one with a scar here." She touched her cheek, drawing a vertical line. "Also, he's holding my purse. I needed two hands to keep myself together long enough to get in here or I would have texted him to come help me."

"Got it. I'll be right back."

* * *

Mikolas stood with the back of his hand pressed to a scotch on the rocks. So much for behaving mainstream and law-abiding, he thought dourly.

He was watching for Viveka, still worried about her. When she had apologized, he'd been floored, already kicking himself for bringing her downstairs at all. He could be at home making love to her, none of this having happened. Instead, he'd let her be terrorized.

There she was. He tried to catch her eye, but she scanned the room, then made for a small group in the far corner from the band.

Mikolas swore under his breath as she approached his target: Aleksy Dmitriev. The Russian magnate had logistics interests that crossed paths with his own from the Aegean through to the Black Sea. Dmitriev had never once returned Mikolas's calls and it grated. He hated being the petitioner and resented the other man for relegating him to that role.

Mikolas knew why Dmitriev was avoiding him. He was scrupulous about his reputation. He wouldn't risk sullying it by attaching himself to the Petrides name.

While Mikolas knew working with Dmitriev would be another seal of legitimacy for his own organization. That's why he wanted to partner with him.

Dmitriev stared at Viveka like she was from Mars, then handed her his drink. He removed his tiepin, handed it to her, then took back his glass. When she asked him something else, he nodded at a window

ledge where a pocketbook sat. Viveka scooped it up and headed back to the ladies' room.

What the *hell*?

Viveka was thankful for the small drama that Clair had provided, but flashed right back to seesaw emotions when she returned to Mikolas's side. He stood out without trying. He wore that look of disinterest that alpha wolves wore with their packs, confident in his superiority so with nothing to prove.

A handful of men in sharp suits had clustered around him. They all wore bored-looking women on their arms.

Mikolas interrupted the conversation when she arrived. He took her hand and made a point of introducing her.

She smiled, but the man who'd been speaking was quick to dismiss her and continue what he was saying. He struck her as the toady type who sucked up to powerful men in hopes of catching scraps. The way the women were held like dogs on a leash was very telling, too.

Viveka let her gaze stray to the other groups, seeing the dynamic was very different in Clair's circle, where she was nodding at whoever was speaking, smiling and fully engaged in the conversation. Her husband was looking their way and she pressed a brief smile onto her mouth.

Nothing.

Mikolas had been right about invisible barriers.

"This must be your new bride if the merger has

gone through," one of the other men broke in to say, frowning with confusion as he jumped his gaze between her and Mikolas.

I have a name, Viveka wanted to remind the man, but apparently on this side of the room, she was a "this."

"No," Mikolas replied, offering no further explanation.

Viveka wanted to roll her eyes. It was basic playground etiquette to act friendly if you wanted to be included in the games. That was what he wanted, wasn't it? Was this what he had meant when he had said it was her task to change how he was viewed?

"I stopped the wedding," she blurted. "He was supposed to marry my sister, but…" She cleared her throat as she looked up at Mikolas, laughing inwardly at the ridiculous claim she was about to make. "I fell head over heels. You weren't far behind me, were you?"

Mikolas wore much the same incredulous expression he had when he'd lifted her veil.

"Your sister can't be happy about that," one of the women said, perking up for the first time.

"She's fine with it," Viveka assured with a wave. "She'd be the first to say you should follow your heart, wouldn't she?" she prodded Mikolas, highly entertained with her embellishment on the truth. *Laugh with me*, she entreated.

"Let's dance." His grip on her hand moved to her elbow and he turned her toward the floor. As he took her in his arms seconds later, he said, "I cannot believe you just said that."

"Oh, come on. You said we should appear long-term. Now they think we're in love and by the way, your friends are a pile of sexist jerks."

"I don't have friends," he growled. "Those are people whose names I know."

His touch on her seemed to crackle and spark, making her feel sensitized all over. At the same time, she thought she heard something in his tone that was a warning.

Dancing with him was easy. They moved really well together right out of the gate. She let herself become immersed in the moment, where the music transmitted through them, making them move in unison. He held her in his strong arms and the closeness was deliciously stimulating. Her heart fluttered and she feared she really would tumble into deep feelings for him.

"They should call it heels over head," she said, trying to break the spell. "We're head over heels right now. It means you're upright."

He halted their dance, started to say something, but off to her right, Clair said, "Vivi. Let me introduce you properly. My husband, Aleksy Dmitriev."

Mikolas pulled himself back from a suffocating place where his emotions had knotted up. She'd been joking with all that talk of love, he knew she had, but even having a falsehood put out there to those vultures had made him uncomfortable.

He had been pleased to feel nothing for Trina. He would have introduced her as his wife and the presumption of affection might have been made, but it wouldn't have been true. It certainly wouldn't have been something that could be used to prey on his psyche, not deep down where his soul kept well out of the light.

Viveka was different. Her blasé claim of love between them was an overstatement and he ought to be able to dismiss it. But as much as he wanted to feel nothing toward her, he couldn't. Everything he'd done since meeting her proved to himself that he felt *something*.

He tried to ignore how disarmed that made him feel, concentrating instead on finding himself face-to-face with the man who'd been evading him for two years.

Dmitriev looked seriously peeved, mouth flat and the scar on his face standing out white.

It's the Viveka effect, Mikolas wanted to drawl.

Dmitriev nodded a stiff acknowledgment to Viveka's warm smile.

"Did you think you were being robbed?" Viveka teased him.

"It crossed my mind." Dmitriev lifted a cool gaze to Mikolas. *When I realized she was with you*, he seemed to say.

Mikolas kept a poker face as Viveka finished the introduction, but deep down he waved a flag of triumph over Dmitriev being forced to come to him.

It was only an introduction, he reminded himself.

A hook. There was no reeling in this kind of fish without a fight.

"We have to get back to the children," Clair was saying. "But I wanted to thank you again for your help."

"My pleasure. I hope we'll run into each other in future," Viveka said. Mikolas had to give her credit. She was a natural at this role.

"Perhaps you can add us to your donor list," Mikolas said. *I do my homework*, he told Dmitriev with a flick of his gaze. Clair ran a foundation that benefited orphanages across Europe. Mikolas had been waiting for the right opportunity to use this particular door. He had no scruples about walking through it as Viveka's plus one.

"May I?" Clair brightened. "I would love that!"

Mikolas brought out one of his cards and a pen, scrawling Viveka's details on the back, mentally noting he should have some cards of her own printed.

"I'd give you one of mine, but I'm out," Clair said, showing hands that were empty of all but a diamond and platinum wedding band. "I've been talking up my fund-raising dinner in Paris all night—oh! Would you happen to be going there at the end of next month? I could put you on that list, too."

"Please do. I'm sure we can make room," Mikolas said smoothly. *We, our, us.* It was a foreign language to him, but surprisingly easy to pick up.

"I'm being shameless, aren't I?" Clair said to her husband, dipping her chin while lifting eyes filled with playful culpability.

The granite in Dmitriev's face eased to what might pass for affection, but he sounded sincere as he contradicted her. "You're passionate. It's one of your many appealing qualities. Don't apologize for it."

He produced one of his own cards and stole the pen Mikolas still held, wordlessly offering both to his wife.

I see what you're doing, Dmitriev said with a level stare at Mikolas while Clair wrote. Dmitriev was of similar height and build to Mikolas. He was probably the only man in the room whom Mikolas would instinctively respect without testing the man first. He emanated the same air of self-governance that Mikolas enjoyed and had more than demonstrated he couldn't be manipulated into doing anything he didn't want to do.

He provoked all of Mikolas's instincts to dominate, which made getting this man's contact details that much more significant.

But even though he wasn't happy to be giving up his direct number, it was clear by Dmitriev's hard look that it was a choice he made consciously and deliberately—for his wife.

Mikolas might have lost a few notches of regard for the man if his hand hadn't still been throbbing from connecting with Grigor's jaw. Which he'd done for Viveka.

It was an uncomfortable moment of realizing it didn't matter how insulated a man believed himself to be. A woman—one for whom he'd gone heels over head—could completely undermine him.

Which was why Mikolas firmed himself against letting Viveka become anything more than the sexual infatuation she was. The only reason he was bent out of shape was because they hadn't had sex yet, he told himself. Once he'd had her, and anticipation was no longer clouding his brain, he'd be fine.

"That was what we came for," he said, after the couple had departed. He indicated the card Viveka was about to drop into her pocketbook. "We can leave now, too."

Mikolas made a face at the card the doorman handed him on their way in, explaining he was supposed to call the police in the morning to make a statement. They didn't speak until they were in the penthouse.

"I've wanted Dmitriev's private number for a while. You did well tonight," he told her as he moved to pour two glasses at the bar.

"It didn't feel like I did anything," she murmured, quietly glowing under his praise. She yearned for approval more than most people did, having been treated as an annoyance for most of her early years.

"It's easy for you. You don't mind talking to people," he remarked, setting aside the bottle and picking up the glasses to come across and offer hers. "Do you take yours with water?"

"I haven't had ouzo in years," she murmured, trying to hide her reaction to him by inhaling the licorice aroma off the alcohol. "I shouldn't have had it when I did. I was far too young. *Yiamas.*"

Mikolas threw most of his back in one go, eyes never leaving hers.

"What, um…?" Oh, this man easily emptied her brain. "You, um, don't like talking to people? You said you hated those sorts of parties."

"I do," he dismissed.

"Why?"

"Many reasons." He shrugged, moving to set aside his glass. "My grandfather had a lot to hide when I first came to live with him. I was too young to be confident in my own opinions and didn't trust anyone with details about myself. As an adult, I'm surrounded by people who are so superficial, crying about ridiculous little trials, I can't summon any interest in whatever it is they're saying."

"Should I be complimented that you talk to me?" she teased.

"I keep trying not to." Even that was delivered with self-deprecation tilting his mouth.

Her heart panged. She longed to know everything about him.

His gaze fixed on her collarbone. He reached out to take her hair back from her shoulder. "You've had one sparkle of glitter here all night," he said, fingertip grazing the spot.

It was a tiny touch, an inconsequential remark, but it devastated her. Her insides trembled and she went very still, her entire being focused on the way he ever so lightly tried to coax the fleck off her skin.

Behind him, the lamps cast amber reflections against the black windows. The pool glowed a ghostly blue on the deck beyond. It made radiance seem to emanate from him, but maybe that was her foolish, dampening eyes.

Painful yearning rose in her. It was familiar, yet held a searing twist. For a long time she had wanted a man in her life. She wanted a confidant, someone she could kiss and touch and sleep beside. She wanted intimacy, physical and emotional.

She had never expected this kind of corporeal desire. She hadn't believed it existed, definitely hadn't known it could overwhelm her like this.

How could she feel so attracted and needy toward a man who was so ambivalent toward her? It was excruciating.

But when he took her glass and set it aside, she didn't resist. She kept holding his gaze as his hands came up to frame her face. And waited.

His gaze lowered to her lips.

They felt like they plumped with anticipation.

She looked at his mouth, not thinking about anything except how much she wanted his kiss. His lips were so beautifully shaped, full, but undeniably masculine. The tip of his tongue wet them, then he lowered his head, came closer.

The first brush of his damp lips against hers made her shudder in release of tension while tightening with anticipation. She gasped in surrender as his hands whispered down to warm her upper arms, then grazed over the fabric of her dress.

Then his mouth opened wider on hers and it was like a straight shot of ouzo, burning down her center and warming her through, making her drunk. Long, dragging kisses made her more and more lethargic by degrees, until he drew back and she realized her hand was at the back of his head, the other curled into the fabric of his shirt beneath his jacket.

He released her long enough to shrug out of his jacket, loosened his tie, then pulled her close again.

Her head felt too heavy for her neck, easily falling into the fingers that combed through her hair and splayed against her scalp. He kissed her again, harder this time, revealing the depth of passion in him. The aggression. It was scary in the way thunder and high winds and landslides were both terrifying and awe-inspiring. She clung to him, moaning in submission. Not just to him, but to her own desire.

They shuffled their feet closer, sealing themselves one against the other, trying to press through clothing and skin so their cells would weave into a single being.

The thrust of his aroused flesh pressed into her stomach and a wrench of conflict went through her. This moment was too perfect. It felt too good to be held like this, to ruin it with humiliating confessions about her defect and entreaties for special treatment. She felt too much toward him, not least gratitude and wonder and a regard that was tied to his compliments and his protection and his hand dragging her to the surface of the water before he'd even known her name.

She ached to share something with him, had since almost the first moment she'd seen him. *Be careful*, she told herself. Sex was powerful. She was already very susceptible to him.

But she couldn't make herself stop touching him. Her hands strayed to feel his shape, tracing him through his pants. It was a bold move for her, but she was entranced. Curious and enthralled. There was a part of her that desperately wanted to know she could please a man, *this* man in particular.

His breath hissed in and his whole body hardened. He gathered his muscles as if he was preparing to dip and lift her against his chest.

She drew back.

His arms twitched in protest, but he let her look at where his erection pressed against the front of his suit pants. He was really aroused. She licked her lips, not superconfident in what she wanted to do, but she wanted to do it.

She unbuckled his belt.

His hands searched under the fall of her hair. His touch ran down her spine, releasing the back of her dress.

As the cool air swirled from her waist around to her belly, her stomach fluttered with nerves. She swallowed, aware of her breasts as her bodice loosened and shifted against her bare nipples. She shivered as his fingertips stroked her bare back. Her hands shook as she pulled his shirt free and clumsily opened his buttons, then spread the edges wide so she could admire his chest.

Pressing her face to his taut skin, she rubbed back and forth and back again, absorbing the feel of him with her brow and lips, drawing in his scent, too moved to smile when he said something in a tight voice and slid his palm under her dress to brand her bottom with his hot palm.

Her mouth opened of its own accord, painting a wet path to his nipple. She explored the shape with her tongue, earned another tight curse, then hit the other one with a draw of her mouth. Foreplay and foreshadowing, she thought with a private smile.

"Bedroom," he growled, bringing his hands out of her dress and setting them on her waist, thumbs against her hip bones as he pressed her back a step.

Dazed at how her own arousal was climbing, Viveka smiled, pleased to see the glitter in his eyes and the flush on his cheeks. It increased her tentative confidence. She placed her hands on his chest and let her gaze stray past him to the armchair, silently urging him toward it.

Mikolas let her have her way out of sheer fascination. He refused to call it weakness, even though he was definitely under a spell of some kind. He had known there was a sensual woman inside Viveka screaming to get out. He hadn't expected this, though.

It wasn't manipulation, either. There were no sly smiles or knowing looks as she slid to her knees between his, kissing his neck, stroking down his front so his abdominals contracted under her tickling fingertips. She was focused and enthralled, timid but genuinely excited. It was erotic to be wanted like this. Beyond exciting.

As she finished opening his pants, his brain shorted out. He was vaguely aware of lifting his hips so she could better expose him. The sob of want that left her was the kind of siren call that had been the downfall of ancient seamen. He nearly exploded on the spot.

He was thick and aching, so hot he wanted to rip his clothes from his body, but he was transfixed. He gripped the armrest in his aching hand and the back of the chair over his shoulder with the other, trying to hold on to his control.

He shouldn't let her do this, he thought distantly. His discipline was in shreds. But therein lay her power. He couldn't make himself stop her. That was the naked truth.

She took him in hand, her touch light, her pale hands pretty against the dark strain of his flesh. He was so hard he thought he'd break, so aroused he couldn't breathe, and so captivated, he could only hold still and watch through slitted eyes as her head dipped.

He groaned aloud as her hair slid against his exposed skin and her wet mouth took him in, narrowing his world to the tip of his sex. It was the most exquisite sensation, nearly undoing him between one breath and the next. She kept up the tender, lascivious act until he was panting, barely able to speak.

"I can't hold back," he managed to grit out.

Slowly her head lifted, pupils huge as pansies in the dim light, mouth swollen and shiny like he'd been kissing her for hours.

"I don't want you to." Her hot breath teased his

wet flesh, tightening all his nerve endings, pulling him to a point that ended where her tongue flicked out and stole what little remained of his willpower.

He gave himself up to her. This was for both of them, he told himself. He would have staying power after this. He'd make it good for her, as good as this. Nothing could be better, but at least this good—

The universe exploded and he shouted his release to the ceiling.

CHAPTER NINE

VIVEKA HUGGED THE front of her gaping dress to her breasts and could barely meet her own glassy eyes in the mirror. She was flushed and aroused and deeply self-conscious. She couldn't believe what she'd just done, but she had no regrets. She had enjoyed giving Mikolas pleasure. It had been extraordinary.

She had needed that for herself. She wasn't a failure in the bedroom after all. Okay, the lounge, she allowed with a smirk.

Her hand trembled as she removed the pins from her hair, pride quickly giving way to sexual frustration and embarrassment. Even a hint of desolation. If she wasn't such a freak, if she wasn't afraid she'd lose herself completely, they could have found release together.

Being selfless was satisfying in other ways, though. He might be thanking her for breaking up the wedding and saving him a few bucks, but she was deeply grateful for the way he had acknowledged her as worth saving, worth protecting.

The bathroom door that she'd swung almost closed pushed open, making her heart catch.

Mikolas took up a lazy pose that made carnal hunger clench mercilessly in her middle. The flesh that was hot with yearning squeezed and ached.

His open shirt hung off his shoulders, framing the light pattern of hair that ran down from his breastbone. His unfastened pants gaped low across his hips, revealing the narrow line of hair from his navel. His eyelids were heavy, disguising his thoughts, but his voice was gritty enough to make her shiver.

"You're taking too long."

The words were a sensual punch, flushing her with eager heat. At the same time, alarm bells—anxious clangs of performance anxiety—went off within her, cooling her ardor.

"For?" She knew what he meant, but she'd taken care of his need. They were done. Weren't they? If she'd ever had sex before, she wouldn't be so unsure.

"Finishing what you started."

"You did finish. You can't—" Was he growing hard again? It looked like his boxers were straining against the open fly of his pants.

She read. She knew basic biology. She knew he'd climaxed, so how was that happening? Was she really so incapable of gratifying a man that even oral sex failed to do the job?

"You can't… Men don't…again. Can they?" She trailed off, blushing and hating that his first real smile came at the expense of her inexperience.

"I'll last longer this time," he promised drily. "But I don't want to wait. Get your butt in that bed, or I'll have you here, bent over the sink."

Oh, she was never going to be that spontaneous. Ever. And for a first time? While he talked about lasting a *long* time?

"No." She hitched the shoulder of her dress and reached behind herself to close it. "You finished. We're done." Her face was on fire, but inside she was growing cold.

He straightened off the doorjamb. "What?"

"I don't want to have sex." Not entirely true. She longed to understand the mystique behind the act, but his talk of sink-bending only told her how far apart they were in experience. The more she thought about it, the more she went into a state of panic. Not him. Not tonight when she was already an emotional mess.

She struggled to close her zip, then crossed her arms, taking a step backward even though he hadn't moved toward her.

He frowned. "You don't want sex?"

Was he deaf?

"No," she assured him. Her back came up against the towel rail, which was horribly uncomfortable. She waved toward the door he was blocking. "You can go."

He didn't move, only folded his own arms and rocked back on his heels. "Explain this to me. And use small words, because I don't understand what happened between the lounge and here."

"Nothing happened." She couldn't stand that he was making her wallow in her inadequacy. "You... I mean, I *thought* I gave you what you wanted. If you thought—"

He didn't even want her. Not really. He would decide *if* and *when*, she recalled.

Good luck with that, champ. Her body made that decision for everyone involved, no matter what her head said.

Do not cry. Oh, she hated her body right now. Her stupid, dumb body that had made her life go so far sideways she didn't even understand how she was standing here having this awful conversation.

"Can you just go?" She glared at him for making this so hard for her, but her eyes stung. She bet they were red and pathetic looking. If he made her tell him, and he laughed— *"Please?"*

He stayed there one more long moment, searching her gaze, before slowly moving back, taking the door with him, closing it as he left. The click sounded horribly final.

Viveka stepped forward and turned the lock, not because she was afraid he'd come in looking for sex, but afraid he'd come in and catch her crying.

With a wrench of her hand, she started the shower.

Mikolas was sitting in the dark, nursing an ouzo, when he heard Viveka's door open.

He'd closed it himself an hour ago, when he'd gone in to check on her and found her on the guest bed, hair wrapped in a towel, one of his monogramed robes swallowing her in black silk. She'd been fast asleep, her very excellent legs bare to midthigh, a crumpled tissue in her lax grip. Several more had been balled up around her.

Rather than easing his mind, rather than answering any of the million questions crowding his thoughts, the sight had caused the turmoil inside him to expand, spinning in fresh and awful directions. Was he such a bad judge of a woman's needs? Why did he feel as though he'd taken advantage of her? She had pressed him into this very chair. She had opened his pants. She had gone down and told him to let go.

He'd been high as a kite when he had tracked her into her bathroom, certain he'd find her naked and waiting for him. Every red blood cell he possessed had been keening with anticipation.

It hadn't gone that way at all.

She'd felt threatened.

He was a strong, dominant man. He knew that and tried to take his aggressive nature down a notch in the bedroom. He knew what it was like to be brutalized by someone bigger and more powerful. He would never do that to the smaller and weaker.

He kept having flashes of slender, delicate Viveka looking anxious as she noticed he was still hard. He thought about her fear of Grigor. A libido-killing dread had been tying his stomach in knots ever since.

He couldn't bear the idea of her being abused that way. He'd punched Grigor tonight, but he wished he had killed him. There was still time, he kept thinking. He wasn't so far removed from his bloodline that he didn't know how to make a man disappear.

He listened to Viveka's bare feet approach, thinking he couldn't blame her for trying to sneak out on him.

She paused as she arrived at the end of the hall, obviously noticing his shadowed figure. She had changed into pajamas and clipped up her hair. She tucked a stray wisp behind her ear.

"I'm hungry. Do you want toast?" She didn't wait for his response, charging past him through to the kitchen.

He unbent and slowly made his way into the kitchen behind her.

She had turned on the light over the stove and kept her back to him as she filled the kettle at the sink. After she set the switch to Boil, she went to the freezer and found a frozen loaf of sliced bread.

Still keeping her back to him, she broke off four slices and set them in the toaster.

"Viveka."

Her slender back flinched at the sound of his voice.

So did he. The things he was thinking were piercing his heart. He'd been bleeding internally since the likeliest explanation had struck him hours ago. When someone reacted that defensively against sexual contact, the explanation seemed really obvious.

"When you said Grigor abused you..." He wasn't a coward, but he didn't want to speak it. Didn't want to hear it. "Did he...?" His voice failed him.

Viveka really wished he hadn't still been up. In her perfect world, she never would have had to face him again, but as the significance of his broken question struck her, she realized she couldn't avoid telling him.

She buried her face in her hands. "No. That's not it. Not at all."

She *really* didn't want to face him.

But she had to.

Shoulders sagging, she turned and wilted against the cupboards behind her. Her hands stayed against her stinging cheeks.

"Please don't laugh." That's what the one other man she'd told had done. She'd felt so raw it was no wonder she hadn't been able to go all the way with him, either.

She dared a peek at Mikolas. He'd closed a couple of buttons, but his shirt hung loose over his pants. His hair was ruffled, as though his fingers had gone through it a few times. His jaw was shadowed with stubble and he looked tired. Troubled.

"I won't laugh." He hadn't slept, even though it was past two in the morning. For some reason that flipped her heart.

"I wasn't a very happy teenager, obviously," she began. "I did what a lot of disheartened young girls do. I looked for a boy to save me. There was a nice one who didn't have much, but he had a kind heart. I can't say I loved him, not even puppy love, but I liked him. We started seeing each other on the sly, behind Grigor's back. After a while it seemed like the time to, you know, have sex."

The toaster made a few pinging, crackling noises and the kettle was beginning to hiss. She chewed her lip, fully grown and many years past it, but still chagrined.

"I mean, fourteen is criminally young, I realize that. And not having any really passionate feelings for him… It's not a wonder it didn't work."

"Didn't work," he repeated, like he was testing words he didn't know.

She clenched her eyes shut. "He didn't fit. It hurt too much and I made him stop. Please don't laugh," she rushed to add.

"I'm not laughing." His voice was low and grave. "You're telling me you're a virgin? You never tried again?"

"Oh, I did," she said to the ceiling, insides scraped hollow.

She moved around looking for the tea and butter, trying to escape how acutely humiliating this was.

"My life was a mess for quite a while, though. Grigor found out I'd been seeing the boy and that I'd gone to the police about Mum. He kicked me out and I moved to London. *That* was a culture shock. The weather, the city. Aunt Hildy had all these rules. It wasn't until I finished my A levels and was working that I started dating again. There was a guy from work. He was very smooth. I realize now he was a player, but I was quite taken in."

The toast popped and she buttered it, taking her time, spreading right to the edges.

"He laughed when I told him why I was nervous." She scraped the knife in careful licks across the surface of the toast. "He was so determined to be The One. We fooled around a little, but he was always putting this pressure on me to go all the way. I *wanted* to have sex. It's supposed to be great, right?"

Pressure arrived behind her eyes again. She couldn't look at him, but she listened, waiting for his confirmation that yes, all the sex he'd had with his multitude of lovers had been fantastic.

Silence.

"Finally I said we could try, but it really hurt. He said it was supposed to and didn't want to stop. I lost my temper and threw him out. We haven't spoken since."

"Do you still work with him?"

"No. Old job. Long gone." The toast was buttered before her on two plates, but she couldn't bring herself to turn and see his reaction.

She was all cried out, but familiar, hopeless angst cloaked her. She just wanted to be like most people and have sex and like it.

"Are you laughing?" Her voice was thready and filled with the embarrassed anguish she couldn't disguise.

"Not at all." His voice sounded like he was talking from very far away. "I'm thinking that not in a thousand years would I have guessed that. Nothing you do fits with the way other people behave. It didn't make sense that you would give me pleasure and not want anything for yourself. You respond to me. I couldn't imagine why you didn't want sex."

"I *do* want sex," she said, flailing a frustrated hand. "I just don't want it to *hurt*." She finally turned and set his plate of toast on the island, avoiding his gaze.

The kettle boiled, giving her breathing space as she moved to make the tea. When she sat down, she went around the far end of the island and took the farthest stool from where he stood ignoring the toast and tea she'd made for him.

She couldn't make herself take a bite. Her body was hot and cold, her emotions swinging from hope to despair to worry.

"You're afraid I wouldn't stop if we tried." His voice was solemn as he promised, "I would, you know. At any point."

A tentative hope moved through her, but she shook her head. "I don't want to be a project." Her spoon clinked lightly as she stirred the sugar into her tea. "I can't face another humiliating attempt. And yes, I've been to a doctor. There's nothing wrong. I'm just... unusually..." She sighed hopelessly. "Can we stop talking about this?"

He only pushed his hands into his pockets. "I wasn't trying to talk you into anything. Not tonight. Unless you want to," he said in a wry mutter, combing distracted fingers through his hair. "I wouldn't say no. You're not a project, Viveka. I want you rather badly."

"Do you?" She scoffed in a strained voice, reminding him, "You said *you* would decide if and when. That *I* was the only one who wanted sex. I can't help the way I react to you, you know. I might have tried with you tonight if I'd thought it would go well, but..."

Tears came into her eyes. It was silly. She was seriously dehydrated from her crying jags earlier. There shouldn't be a drop of moisture left in her.

"I wanted you to like it," she said, heart raw. "I wanted to know I could, you know, *satisfy* a man, but no. I didn't even get that right. You were still hard and—"

He muttered something under his breath and said, "Are you really that oblivious? You *did* satisfy me. You leveled me. Blew my mind. Reset the bar. I don't have words for how good that was." He sounded aggrieved as he waved toward the lounge. "My desire for you is so strong I was aroused all over again just thinking about doing the same to you. *That's* why I was hard again."

If he didn't look so uncomfortable admitting that, she might have disbelieved him.

"When we were on the yacht, you said you thought it was exciting that I respond to you." Her chest ached as she tried to figure him out. "If the attraction is just as strong for you, why don't you want me to know? Why do you keep—I mean, before we went out tonight, you acted as if you could take it or leave it. It's *not* the same for you, Mikolas. That's why I don't think it would work."

"I never like to be at a disadvantage, Viveka. We had been talking about some difficult things. I needed space."

"But if we're equal in feeling *this* way...? Attracted, I mean, why don't you want me to know that?"

"That's not an advantage, is it?"

His words, that attitude of prevailing without mercy, scraped her down to the bones.

"You'll have to tell me sometime what that's like," she said, dabbing at a crumb and pressing it between her tight lips. "Having the advantage, I mean. Not something I've ever had the pleasure of experiencing. Not something I should want to go to bed with, frankly. So *why do I*?"

He did laugh then, but it was ironic, completely lacking any humor.

"For what it's worth, I feel the same." He walked out, leaving his toast and tea untouched.

Mikolas was trying hard to ignore the way Viveka Brice had turned his life into an amusement park. One minute it was a fun house of distorted mirrors, the next a roller coaster that ratcheted his tension only to throw him down a steep valley and around a corner he hadn't seen.

Home, he kept thinking. It was basic animal instinct. Once he was grounded in his own cave, with the safety of the familiar around him, all the ways that she'd shaken up his world would settle. He would be firmly in control again.

Of course he had to keep his balance in the dizzying teacup of her trim figure appearing in a pair of hip-hugging jeans and a completely asexual T-shirt paired with the doe-eyed wariness that had crushed his chest last night.

He couldn't say he was relieved to hear the details of her sexual misadventures. The idea of her lying naked with other men grated, but at least she hadn't been scarred by the horrifying brutality he'd begun to imagine.

On the other hand, when she had finally opened up, the nakedness in her expression had been difficult to witness. She was tough and brave and earnest and too damned sensitive. Her insecurity had reached into him in a way that antagonism couldn't. The bizarre protectiveness she already inspired in him had flared up, prompting him to assuage her fears, reassure her. He had wound up revealing himself in a way that left him mistrustful and feeling like he'd left a flank unguarded.

Not a comfortable feeling at all.

He hadn't been able to sleep. Much of it had been the ache in his body, craving release in hers. He yearned to *show* her how it could be between them. At the same time, his mind wouldn't stop turning over and over with everything that had happened since she had marched into his life. At what point would she quit pulling the rug out from under him?

"Are you taking me back in time? What is that?" She was looking out the window of the helicopter.

He leaned to see. They were approaching the mansion and the ruins built into the cliff below it.

"That is the tower where you will be imprisoned for the rest of your life." *There* was a solution, he thought.

"Don't quit your day job for comedy."

Her quick rejoinder made humor tug at the corner of his mouth. He was learning she used jokes as a defense, similar to how he was quick to pull rank and impose his control over every situation. The fact she was being cheeky now, when he was in her space, told him she was shoring up her walls against him. That niggled, but wasn't it what he wanted? Distance? Barriers?

"The Venetians built it." He gazed at her clean face so close to his, her naked lips. She smelled like tea and roses and woman. He wanted to eat her alive. "See where the stairs have been worn away by the waves?"

Viveka couldn't take in anything as she felt the warmth off the side of his face and caught the smell of his aftershave. She held herself very still, trying not to react to his closeness, but her lips tingled, longing to graze his jaw and find his mouth. Lock with him in a deep kiss.

"We preserved the ruins as best we could. Given the fortune we spent, we were allowed to build above it."

She forced her gaze to the view, instantly enchanted. What little girl hadn't dreamed of being spirited away to an island castle like in a fairy tale?

The modern mansion at the top of the cliff drew her eye unerringly. The view was never-ending in all directions and the ultracontemporary design was unique and fascinating, sprawling in odd angles that were still perfectly balanced. It was neither imposing nor frivolous. It was solid and sophisticated. Dare she say elegant?

She noticed something on the roof. "Are those solar panels?"

"*Nai*. We also have a field of wind turbines. You can't see them from here. We're planning a tidal generator, too. We only have to finalize the location."

"How ecologically responsible of you." She turned her face and they were practically nose to cheekbone.

He sat back and straightened his cuff.

"I like to be self-sufficient." A tick played at the corner of his mouth.

Under no one's power but his own. She was seeing that pattern very clearly. Should she tell him it made him predictable? she wondered with private humor.

A few minutes later, she followed him into an interior she hadn't expected despite all she'd seen so far of the way he lived. The entrance should have struck her as over the top, with its smooth marble columns and split staircase that went up to a landing overlooking, she was sure, the entire universe.

The design remained spare and masculine, however, the colors subtle and golden in the midday light. Ivory marble and black wrought iron along with accents of Hellenic blue made the place feel much warmer than she expected. As they climbed the stairs, thick fog-gray carpet muffled their steps.

The landing looked to the western horizon.

Viveka paused, experiencing a strange sensation that she was looking back toward a life that was just a blur of memory, no longer hers. Oddly, the idea slid into her heart not like a blade that cut her off from her past, but more like something that caught and anchored her here, tugging her from a sea of turbulence to pin her to this stronghold.

She rubbed her arms at the preternatural shiver that chased up her entire body, catching Mikolas's gaze as he waited for her to follow him up another level.

The uppermost floor was fronted by a lounge that was surrounded by walls of glass shaded by an over-hang to keep out the heat. They were at the very top of the world here. That's how it felt. Like she'd arrived at Mount Olympus, where the gods resided.

There was a hot tub on the veranda along with lounge chairs and a small dining area. She stayed inside, glancing around the open-plan space of a breakfast nook, a sitting area with a fireplace and an imposing desk with two flat monitors with a printer on a cabinet behind it, obviously Mikolas's home of-fice.

As she continued exploring, she heard Mikolas speaking, saying her name. She followed to an open door where a uniformed young man came out. He saw her, nodded and introduced himself as Titus, then disappeared toward the stairs.

She peered into the room. It was Trina's boudoir. Had to be. There were fresh flowers, unlit candles beside the bucket of iced champagne, crystal glasses, a peignoir set draped across the foot of the white bed, and a box of chocolates on a side table. The exterior walls were made entirely out of glass and faced east, which pleased her. She liked waking to sun.

Don't love it, she cautioned herself, but it was hard not to be charmed.

"Oh, good grief," she gasped as Mikolas opened a door to what she had assumed was a powder room. It was actually a small warehouse of prêt-à-porter.

"Did you buy all of Paris for her?" She plucked at the cuff of a one-sleeved evening gown in silver-embroidered lavender. The back wall was covered in shoes. "I hate to tell you this, but my foot is a full size bigger than Trina's."

"One of your first tasks will be to go through all of this so the seamstress can alter where necessary. The shoes can be exchanged." He shrugged one shoulder negligently.

The closet was huge, but way too small with both of them in it.

She tried to disguise her self-consciousness by picking up a shoe. When she saw the designer name, she gently rubbed the shoe on her shirt to erase her fingerprint from the patent leather and carefully replaced it.

"Change for lunch with my grandfather. But don't take too long."

"Where are you going?" she asked, poking her head out to watch him cross to a pair of double doors on the other side of her room, not back to the main part of the penthouse.

"My room." He opened one of the double doors as he reached it, revealing what she thought at first was a private sitting room, but that white daybed had a towel rolled up on the foot of it.

Drawn by curiosity, she crossed to follow him into the bathroom. Except it was more like a high-end

"Of course," she said faintly. "Unless I get lost in the forest on the way back to my room."

My room. Freudian slip. She dropped her gaze to the mosaic in the floor, then walked through her water closet to her room.

It was only as she stood debating a pleated skirt versus a sleeveless floral print dress that the significance of that shared bathroom struck her: he could walk in on her naked. Anytime.

spa. There was an enormous round tub set in a
of glass that arched outward so the illusion for
bather was a soak in midair.

"Wow." She slowly spun to take in the extrav
gance, awestruck when she noted the small fores
that grew in a rock garden under a skylight. A path
of stones led through it to a shower *area* against the
back wall. Nozzles were set into the alcove of tiled
walls, ready to spray from every level and direction,
including raining from the ceiling.

She clapped her hand over her mouth, laughing.

The masculine side of the room was a double sink
and mirror designed along the black-and-white sim-
plistic lines Mikolas seemed to prefer, bracketed by
a discreet door to a private toilet stall that also gave
access to his bedroom. Her side was a reflection of
his, with one sink removed to make way for a makeup
bench and a vanity of drawers already filled with un-
opened cosmetics.

"You live like this," she murmured, closing the
drawer.

"So do you. Now."

Temporarily, she reminded herself, but it was still
like trying to grasp the expanse of the universe. Too
much to comprehend.

A white robe that matched the black ones she'd
already worn hung on a hook. She flipped the lapel
enough to see the monogram, expecting a T and finding an M. She sputtered out another laugh. He was
so predictably possessive!

"Can you be ready in twenty minutes?"

CHAPTER TEN

VIVEKA WASN'T SURE what she expected Mikolas's grandfather to look like. A mafia don from an old American movie? Or like many of the other retired Greek men who sat outside village *kafenions*, maybe wearing a flat cap and a checked shirt, face lined by sun and a hard life in the vineyard or at sea?

Erebus Petrides was the consummate old-world gentleman. He wore a suit as he shared a drink with them before they dined. He had a bushy white mustache and excellent posture despite his stocky weight and the cane he used to walk. He and Mikolas didn't look much alike, but they definitely had the same hammered silver eyes and their voices were two keys of a similar strong, commanding timbre.

Erebus spoke English, but preferred Greek, stretching her to recall a vocabulary she hadn't tested in nine years—something he gently reproached her over. It was a pleasant meal that could have been any "Meet the Parents" occasion as they politely got to know each other. She had to keep reminding herself that the charismatic old man was actually a notorious criminal.

"He seems very nice," she said after Erebus had retired for an afternoon rest.

Mikolas was showing her around the rest of the house. They'd come out to the pool deck where a cabana was set up like a sheikh's tent off to the side and the Ionian Sea gleamed into the horizon.

Mikolas didn't respond and she glanced up to see his mouth give a cynical twitch.

"No?" she prompted, surprised.

"He wouldn't have saved me if I hadn't proven to be his grandson."

Her heart skipped and veered as she absorbed that none of this would have happened. She wouldn't be here and neither would he. They never would have met. *What would have become of that orphaned boy?*

"Do you wish that your mother had told your father about you?"

"She may have. My father was no saint," he said with disparagement. "And there is no point wishing for anything to be different. Accept what is, Viveka. I learned that long ago."

It wasn't anything she didn't see in a pop philosophy meme on her newsfeed every day, but she always resisted that fatalistic view. She took a few steps away from him as though to distance herself from his pessimism.

"If I accepted what I was given, I would still be listening to Grigor call me ugly and useless." She didn't realize her hands became tight fists, or that he had come up behind her, until his warm grip gently forced her to bend her elbow as he lifted her hand.

He looked at her white knuckles poking like sharp teeth. His thumb stroked along that bumpy line.

"You've reminded me of something. Come." He smoothly inserted his thumb to open her fist and kept her hand as he tugged her into the house.

"Where?"

He only pulled her along through the kitchen and down the service stairs into a cool room where he turned on the lights to reveal a gym.

Perhaps the original plans had drawn it up as a wine cellar, but it was as much a professional gym as any that pushed memberships every January. Bike, tread, elliptical. Every type of weight equipment, a heavy bag hanging in the corner, skipping ropes dangling from a hook and padded mats on the floor. It was chilly and silent and smelled faintly of leather and air freshener.

"You'll meet me here every morning at six," he told her.

"Pah," she hooted. "Not likely."

"Say that again and I'll make it five."

"You're serious?" She made a face, silently telling him what she thought of that. "For heaven's sake, why? I do cardio most days, but I prefer to work out in the evening."

"I'm going to teach you to throw a punch. This—" he lifted the hand he still held and reshaped it into a fist again "—can do better. And this—" he touched under her chin, lifting her face and letting his thumb tag the spot on her lip where Grigor's mark had been "—won't happen again. Not without your opponent discovering very quickly that he has picked a fight with the wrong woman."

She had been trying to pretend she wasn't vitally aware of her hand in his. Now he was touching her face, looking into her eyes, standing too close.

Somehow she had thought that giving him pleasure would release some of this sexual tension between them. Now everything they'd confessed made it so much worse. The pull was so much *deeper*. He knew things about her. Intensely personal things.

She drew away, breaking all contact, trying to keep a grip on herself as she took in what he was saying.

"You keep surprising me. I thought you were a hardened…" She cut him a glance of apology. "Criminal. You're actually quite nice, aren't you? Wanting to teach me how to defend myself."

"Everyone who surrounds me is a strength, not a liability. That's all this is."

"Liability." The label winded her, making her look away. It was familiar, but she had hoped there was a growing regard between them. But no. He might be attracted to her sexually, last night might have changed her forever, but she was still that thing he was saddled with.

"Right. Whatever you need me to be, wherever." She fought not to let her smarting show, but from her throat to her navel she burned.

"Do you like feeling helpless?" he demanded.

"No," she choked. This feeling of being at *his* mercy was excruciating.

"Then be here at six prepared to work."

* * *

What had he been thinking? Mikolas asked himself the next morning. This was hell.

Viveka showed up in a pair of clinging purple pants that ended below her knees. The spandex was shiny enough to accent every dip and curve of her trim thighs. Her pink T-shirt came off after they'd warmed up with cardio, revealing the unique landscape of her abdomen. Now she wore only a snug blue sports bra that flattened her modest breasts and showed off her creamy shoulders and chest and flat midriff.

He was so distracted by lust, he would get his lights blacked out for sure.

He would deserve it. And he couldn't even make a pass to slake it. He'd told two of his guards who had come in to use the gym that they could stay. They were spotting each other, grunting over the weights, while Mikolas put his hands on Viveka to adjust her stance and coached her through stepping into a punch. She smelled like shampoo and woman sweat. Like they'd been petting each other into acute arousal.

"You're holding back because you're afraid you'll hurt yourself," he told her when she struck his palm. He stopped her to correct her wrist position and traced up the soft skin of her forearm. "Humans have evolved the bone structure in here to withstand the impact of a punch."

"My bones aren't as big as yours," she protested. "I *will* hurt myself in a real fight. Especially if I don't have this." She held up her arm to indicate where he'd wrapped her hands to protect them.

"You might even break your hand," he told her frankly. "But that's better than losing your life, isn't it? I want you on the heavy bag twice a day for half an hour. Get used to how it feels to connect so you won't hesitate when it counts. Learn to use your left with as much power as the right."

Her brow wrinkled with concentration as she went back to jabbing into his palms. She was taking this seriously, at least.

That earnestness worried him, though. It would be just like her to take it to heart that *she* should protect *him*. He'd blurted out that remark about liability last night because he hadn't wanted to admit that her inability to protect herself had been eating at him from the moment he'd seen Grigor throw her around on the deck of a stranger's yacht.

He'd hurt her feelings, of course. She'd made enough mentions of Grigor's disparagement and her aunt's indifference that he understood Viveka had been made to feel like a burden and was very sensitive to it. That heart of hers was so easily bruised!

The more time he spent with her, the more he could see how utterly wrong they were for each other. He could wind up hurting her quite deeply.

I do want sex. I just don't want it to hurt.

Her jab was off-center, glancing off his palm so she stumbled into him.

"Sorry. I'm getting tired," she said breathlessly.

"I wasn't paying attention," he allowed, helping her find her feet.

Damn it, if he didn't keep his guard up, they were both going to get hurt.

Viveka was still shaking from the most intense workout of her life. Her arms felt like rubber and she needed the seamstress's help to dress as they worked through the gowns in her closet. She would have consigned Mikolas firmly to hell for this morning's punishment, but then his grandfather's physiotherapist arrived on Mikolas's instruction to offer her a massage.

"He said you would need one every day for at least a week."

Viveka had collapsed on the table, groaned with bliss and went without prompting back to the gym that afternoon to spend another half hour on the wretched heavy bag.

"You'll get used to it," Mikolas said without pity at dinner, when she could barely lift her fork.

"Surely that's not necessary, is it?" Erebus admonished Mikolas, once his grandson had explained why Viveka was so done in.

"She wants to learn. Don't you?" Mikolas's tone dared her to contradict him, but he wasn't demanding she agree with him in front of his grandfather. He was insisting on honesty.

"I do," she admitted with a weighted sigh, even though the very last thing she ever wanted was to engage in a fistfight. She couldn't help wondering if

Grigor would have been as quick to hit her if she'd ever hit him back, though. She'd never had the nerve, fearing she'd only make things worse.

Mikolas's treatment of her in the gym, as dispassionate as it had been, had also been heartening. He seemed to have every confidence in her ability to defend herself if she only practiced. That was an incredibly compelling thought. Empowering.

It made her grateful to him all over again. And yes, deep down, it made her want to make him proud. To show him what she was capable of. Show herself.

Of course, the other side of that desire to be plucky and capable was a churning knowledge that she was being a coward when it came to sex. She wanted to be proficient in that arena, too.

The music was on low when they came into the lounge of his penthouse later, the fire glowing and a bottle of wine and glasses waiting. Beyond the windows, stars sparkled in the velvet black sky and moonlight glittered on the sea.

Had he planned this? To seduce her?

Did she want to be seduced?

She sighed a little, not sure what she wanted anymore.

"Sore?" he asked, moving to pour the wine.

"Hmm? Oh, it's not that bad. The massage helped. No, I was just thinking that I'm stuck in a holding pattern."

He lifted his brows with inquiry.

"I thought once Hildy was sorted, I would begin taking my life in hand. Trina was supposed to come live with me. I had some plan that we would rent a flat and take online quizzes, choose a career and register for classes…" She had been looking forward to that, but her sister's life had skewed off from hers and she didn't even have the worry of Hildy any longer. "Instead, my future is a blank page."

On Petrides letterhead, she thought wryly.

"I'll figure it out," she assured herself. "Eventually. I won't be here forever, right?"

That knowledge was the clincher. If it had taken her twenty-three years to find a man who stirred her physically, how long would it take to find another?

She looked over to him.

Whatever was in her face made him set down the bottle, corkscrew angled into the unpopped cork.

"I keep telling myself to give you time." His voice was low and heavy, almost defeated. "But bringing you into my bed is all I can think about. Will you let me? I just want to touch you. Kiss you. Give you what you gave me."

Her belly clenched in anticipation. She couldn't imagine being *that* uninhibited, but she couldn't imagine *not* going to bed with him. She wanted him *so much* and she honestly didn't know how to resist any longer.

Surrender happened with one shaken, "Yes."

He kind of jolted, like he hadn't expected that. Then he came across and took her face in his two hands, covering her lips with his hot, hungry mouth. They kissed like lovers. Like people who had been separated by time and distance and deep misunderstanding. She curled her arms around his neck and he broke away long enough to scoop her up against his chest, then kissed her again as he carried her to his bedroom.

She waited for misgivings and none struck. Her fingers went into his hair as she kissed him back.

He came down on the mattress with her and she opened her eyes only long enough to catch an impression of monochromatic shades lit by the bluish half-moon. The carpet was white, the furniture silver-gray, the bedspread black.

Then Mikolas tucked her beneath him and stroked without hurry from her shoulder, down her rib cage, past her waist and along her hip.

"You can—" she started to say, but he brushed another kiss over her lips, lazy and giving and thorough.

"Don't worry," he murmured and kissed her again. "I just want to touch you." Another soft, sweet, lingering kiss. "I'll stop if you tell me to." Kissing and kissing and kissing.

It was delicious and tender and not the least bit threatening with his heavy hand only making slow, restless circles where her hip met her waist.

She wanted more. She wanted sex. It wasn't like the other times she'd wanted sex. Then it had been something between an obligation and a frustrating goal she was determined to achieve.

This was nothing like that. She wanted *him*. She wanted to share her body with Mikolas, feel him inside her, feel close to him.

Make love to me, she begged him with her lips,

and ran her hands over him in a silent message of encouragement. When she rolled and tried to open the zip on her dress, he made a ragged noise and found it for her, dragging it down. He lifted away to draw her sleeve off her arm, exposing her bra. One efficient flick of his fingers and the bra was loose.

With reverence, he eased the strap down her arm, dislodging the cup so her breast thrust round and white, nipple turgid with wanton need.

Insecurity didn't have time to strike. He lowered his head and tongued lightly, cupped with a warm hand, then with another groan of appreciation, opened his mouth in a hot branding, letting her get used to the delicate suction before pulling a little harder.

Her toes curled. She wanted to speak, to tell him this was good, that he wouldn't have to stop, but sensation rocked her, coiling in her abdomen, making her loins weep with need. When his hand stroked to rub her bottom, she dragged at her skirt herself, earning a noise of approval as she drew the ruffled fabric out of the way.

He teased her, tracing patterns on her bare thighs, lifting his head to kiss her again and give her his tongue as he made her wait and wait.

"Mikolas," she gasped.

"This?" He brought his hand to the juncture of her thighs and settled his palm there, letting her get used to the sensation. The intimacy. "I want that, too," he breathed against her mouth.

She bit back a cry of pure joy as the weight of his hand covered her, hot and confident. He rocked slowly, increasing the pressure in increments, inciting her to crook her knee so she was open to his touch. Eyes closed, she let herself bask in this wonderful feeling, tension climbing.

When he lifted his hand, she caught her breath in loss, opening her eyes.

He was watching her while his fingertips traced the edge of her knickers, then began to draw them down her thighs.

The friction of lace against her sensitized skin made her shiver. As the coolness of the room struck her damp, eager flesh, she became starkly aware of how her clothing was askew, her breast exposed, her sex pouted and needy, her body trembling with ridiculously high desire.

For a moment anxiety struck. She wanted to rush past this moment, rush through the hard part, have done with this interminable impasse. She lifted her hips so he could finish skimming them away, but when he came down beside her again, he only combed her hair back from her face.

"I just want to feel you. I'll be gentle," he promised, and kissed her lightly.

Yes, she almost screamed.

Embarrassment ought to be killing her, but arousal was pulsing in her like an electrical current. And when he cradled her against him this way, she felt very safe.

They kissed and his hand covered her again. This time she was naked. The sensation was so acute she jolted under his touch.

"Just feel," he cajoled softly. "Tell me what you like. Is that good?"

He did things then that were gorgeous and honeyed. She knew how her body worked, but she had never felt this turned on. She didn't let herself think, just floated in the deep currents of pleasure he swirled through her.

"Like that?" He kept up the magical play, making tension coil through her so she moaned beneath his kiss, encouraging him. Yes, like that. Exactly like that.

He pressed one finger into her.

She gasped.

"Okay?" he breathed against her cheek.

She clasped him with her inner muscles, loving the sensation even though it felt very snug. She was so aroused, so close, she covered his hand with her own and pressed. She rocked her hips as he made love to her with his hand and shattered into a million pieces, cries muffled by his smothering kiss.

CHAPTER ELEVEN

THEY WERE GOING to kill each other.

Mikolas was fully clothed and if she shaped him through his pants right now, he would explode.

But oh, she was amazing. He licked at her panting lips, wanting to smile at the way she clung to his mouth with her own, but weakly. She was still shivering with the aftershocks of her beautiful, stunning orgasm.

He caressed her very, very gently, coaxing her to remain aroused. He wanted to do that to her again. Taste her. Drown in her.

She made a noise and kissed him back with more response, restless hands picking at his shirt, looking for the buttons.

He broke them open with a couple of yanks, then shrugged it off and discarded it, too hot for clothes. On fire for her.

She pulled her other arm free of her dress and held up her arms for him to come back. Soft curves, velvety skin. He loved the feel of her against his bare chest and biceps. Delicate, but spry. So warm, smelling of rain and tea and the drugging scent of sexual fulfillment.

Her smooth hands traced over his torso and back, making him groan at how good it felt on skin that was taut and sensitized. She tasted like nectarines, he thought, opening his mouth on the swell of her breast. He tongued her nipple, more aggressive than he had been the first time.

She arched for more.

He was going too fast, he cautioned himself, but he wanted to consume her. He wanted her dress out of the way, he wanted her hands everywhere on him—

She arched to strip the garment down.

He slid down the bed as he whisked the dress away, pressing his lips to her quivering belly, blowing softly on the fine hairs of her mound, laughing with delight at finally being here. He was so filled with desire his heart was slamming, pulse reverberating through his entire body.

"Mikolas," she breathed.

Her fingers were in his hair like she was petting a wolf, tugging hard enough to force him to lift his head before he'd barely nuzzled her.

"Make love to me."

A lightning rod of lust went through him. He steeled himself to maintain his control when all he wanted was to push her legs apart and rise over her.

"I am." He was going to make her scream with release.

"I mean really." Her hand moved to cradle his jaw,

her touch light against the clenched muscle in his cheek. Entreaty filled her eyes. "Please."

She had come into his life to destroy him in the most subversive yet effective way possible.

He could barely move, but he drew back, coming up on an elbow, trying to hold on to what shreds of gentlemanly conduct he possessed.

"Do you ever do what's expected of you?"

"You don't want to?" The appalled humiliation that crept into her tone scared the hell out of him.

"Of course I *want* to." He spoke too harshly. He was barely hanging on to rational thought over here.

She tensed, wary.

He set his hand on her navel, breathed, tried to find something that passed for civilized behavior, but found only the thief he had once been. His hand stole lower, unable to help himself. His thumb detoured along her cleft, finding her slick and ready. Need pearled into one place that made her gasp raggedly when he found it, circling and teasing.

Her thighs relaxed open. She arched to his touch. "Please," she begged. "I want to know how it feels."

He was only human, not a superhero. He pulled away, hearing her catch back a noise of injury.

Her breath caught in the next instant as she saw he was rising to open his pants. He stripped in jerky, uncoordinated movements, watching her swallow and bite her bottom lip. He made himself take his time retrieving the condom so she had lots of opportunity to change her mind.

"I'll stop if you want me to," he promised as he

covered himself, then settled over her. He would. He didn't know how, but he would.

Please don't make me stop.

It would really happen this time. Viveka's nerves sizzled as Mikolas covered her. He was such a big person compared with her. He *loomed*. She skimmed her fingertips over his broad shoulders and was starkly aware of how much space his hips and thighs took up as he settled without hesitation between her own.

She tensed, nervous.

He kissed her in abbreviated catches of her mouth that didn't quite satisfy before he pulled away, then did it again.

She made a noise of impatience and wiggled beneath him. "I want—"

"Me, too," he growled against her mouth. Then he lifted to trace himself against her folds. "You're sure?" he murmured, looking down to where they touched.

So sure. "Yes," she breathed.

He positioned himself and pressed.

It hurt. So much. She fought her instinctive tension, tried to make herself relax, tried not to resist, but the sting became more and more intense. He seemed huge. Tears came into her eyes. She couldn't hold back a throaty noise of anxiety.

He stilled, shuddering. The sting subsided a little.

"Viveka." His voice was ragged. "That's just the tip—" He hung his head against her shoulder, forehead damp with perspiration, big body shaking.

"Don't stop." She caught her foot behind his thigh and tried to press him forward.

"*Glykia mou*, I don't want to hurt you." He lifted his face and wore a tortured expression.

"That's why it's okay if you do." Her mouth quivered, barely able to form words. It still hurt, but she didn't care. "I trust you. Please don't make me do this with someone else."

He bit out a string of confounded curses, looking into the shadows for a moment. Then he met her gaze and carefully pressed again.

She couldn't help flinching. Tensing. The stretch hurt a lot. He paused again, looked at her with as much frustration as she felt.

"Don't try to be gentle. Just do it," she told him.

He wavered, then made a tight noise of angst, covered her mouth, gathered himself and thrust deep.

She arched at the flash of pain, crying out into his mouth.

They both stayed motionless for a few hissing breaths.

Slowly the pain eased to a tolerable sting. She moved her lips against his and he kissed her gently. Sweetly.

"Do you hate me?" His voice was thick, his brow tense as he set it against hers. His expression was strained.

He didn't move, letting her get used to the feel of a man inside her for the first time. And he held her in such protective arms, her eyes grew wet from the complete opposite of pain: happiness.

She returned his healing kiss with one that was a little more inciting.

"No," she answered, smiling shakily, feeling intensely close to him. She let her arms settle across his back and traced the indent of his spine, enjoying the way he reacted with a shiver.

"Want to stop?" he asked.

"No." Her voice was barely there. Tentatively she moved a little, settling herself more comfortably beneath him. "I'm not sure I want you to move at all," she admitted wryly. "Ever."

His breath released on a jagged chuckle. "You are going to be the death of me."

Very carefully, he shifted so he was angled on his elbow, then he made a gentling noise and touched where they were joined.

"You feel so good," he crooned in Greek, gently soothing and stimulating as he murmured compliments. "I thought nothing could be better than the way you took me apart with your mouth, but this feels incredible. You're so perfect, Viveka. So lovely."

The noise that escaped her then was pure pleasure. He was leading her down the road of stirred desire to real excitement. It felt strange to have him lodged inside her while her arousal intensified. Part of her wanted him to move, but she was still wary of the pain and this felt so good. The way he stretched her accentuated the sensations. She grew taut and deeply aroused. Restless and—

"Oh, Mikolas. Please. Oh—" A powerful climax rocked her. Her sheath clenched and shivered around his hard shape with such power she could hardly breath. Stars imploded behind her eyes and she clung to him, crying out with ecstasy. It was beautiful and selfish and heavenly.

As the spasms faded, he began to pull away. The friction felt good, except sharp. She wasn't sure she could take that in a prolonged way, but then he was gone from her body and she was bereft.

"You didn't, did you?" She reached to find his thick shaft, so hard and hot, obviously unsatisfied.

He folded his hand over hers and pumped into her fist. Two, three times, then he pressed a harsh groan into her shoulder, mouth opening so his teeth sat against her skin, not quite biting while he shuddered and pulsed against her palm.

Shocked, but pleased, she continued to pleasure him until he relaxed and released her. He removed the condom with a practiced twist, then rolled away and sat up to discard it. Before he came back, he dragged the covers down and pulled her with him as he slid under them.

"Why did you do that?" she asked as he molded her to his front, stomach to stomach.

"So we won't be cold while we sleep." He adjusted the edge of the sheet away from her face.

"You know what I mean." She pinched his chest, unable to lie still when it felt so good to rub her naked legs against his and nuzzle his collarbone with her lips.

"Learn to speak plainly when we're in bed," he ordered.

"Or what?" She was giddy, so happy with being his lover she felt like the sun was lodged inside her.

"Or I may not give you what you want."

They were both silent a moment, bodies quieting.

"You did," she said softly, adjusting her head against his shoulder. "Thank you."

He didn't say anything, but his hand moved thoughtfully in her hair.

A frozen spike of insecurity pierced her. "Did *you* like it?"

He snorted. "I have just finessed my way through initiating a particularly delicate virgin. My ego is so enormous right now, it's a wonder you fit in the bed."

Viveka woke to an empty bed, couldn't find Mikolas in the penthouse, realized she was late for the gym and decided she was entitled to a bath. She was climbing out of it, a thick white towel loosely clutched around her middle, when he strolled in wearing his gym shorts and nothing else.

"Lazy," he stated, pausing to give her a long, appreciative look.

"Seriously?" Before that bath, she had ached *everywhere*.

His mouth twitched and he came closer, gaze skimming down her front. "Sore?"

She shrugged a shoulder, instantly so shy she nearly couldn't bear it. The things they'd done!

She blushed, aware that her gaze was coveting the hard planes of his body, and instantly wanted to be close to him. Touch, feel, kiss…more.

She wasn't sure how to issue the invitation across the expanse of the spa-like bathroom, but he wasn't the novice she was. He took the last few laconic steps to reach her, spiky lashes lowering as he stared at her mouth. When his head dipped, she lifted her chin to meet his kiss. Her free hand found his stubbled cheek while her other kept her towel in place.

"Mmm..." she murmured, liking the way he didn't rush, but kissed her slowly and thoroughly.

He drew back and tried taking the towel in his two hands.

She hesitated.

"I only want a peek," he cajoled.

"It's daylight," she argued.

"Exactly."

If she had feared that having sex would weaken her will around him, the fear was justified. She wanted to please him. She wanted to offer her whole self and plead with him to cherish her. Her fingers relaxed under the knowledge she was giving up more than control of a towel.

As he opened it, however, and took a long eyeful of her sucked-in stomach and thrust-out breasts, she saw desire grip him with the same lack of mercy it showed her. He swallowed, body hardening, jaw clenched like he was under some kind of deep stress.

"I was only going to kiss you," he said, lifting lust-filled eyes to hers. "But if you—"

"I do," she assured him.

He let the towel drop and she met him midway, moaning with acquiescence as he pressed her onto the daybed. Her inhibitions about the daylight quickly burned up as his stubble slid down her neck to her breast where he sucked and made her writhe. When he slid even lower, scraping her stomach then her thighs as he knelt on the floor, she threw her arm across her eyes and let him do whatever he wanted.

Because it was what she wanted. Oh, that felt exquisite.

"Don't stop," she pleaded when he lifted his head.

"Can you take me?" he growled, scraping his teeth with mock threat along her inner thigh.

She nodded, little echoes of wariness threatening, but she couldn't take her eyes off his form as he rose and moved to the mirror over his sink, found a condom and covered himself.

When he came back and stood over her, she stayed exactly as he'd left her, splayed weakly with desire, like some harem girl offered for his pleasure.

His hands flexed like he was struggling against some kind of internal pain.

"Mikolas," she pleaded, holding out her arms.

He made a noise of agony and came down over her, heavy and confident, thighs pressing hers wide as he positioned himself. "I don't want to hurt you." His hand tangled in her hair. "But I want you so damned much. Stop me if it hurts."

"It's okay," she told him, not caring about the burn as she arched, inviting him to press all the way in. It hurt, but his first careful thrusts felt good at the same time. The friction of him moving inside her made the connection that much more intense. She rose to the brink very quickly, climaxing with a sudden gasp, clinging to him, shocked at her reaction.

He shuddered, lips pressed into her neck, and hurried to finish with her, groaning fulfillment against her skin.

She was disappointed when he carefully disengaged and sat up, his back to her.

She started to protest that it was okay, holding him in her didn't hurt anymore, but she was distracted by the marks on his back. They were pocked scars that were visible only because the light was so bright. She'd seen his back on the yacht, but in lamplight she hadn't noticed the scars. They weren't raised, but there were more than a dozen.

"What happened to your back?" she asked, puzzled.

Mikolas rose and walked first to his side of the room, where he scanned around his sinks, then went across to her vanity, where he found the remote for the shower.

"We should set some ground rules," he said.

"Leave the remote on your side?" she guessed as she rose. She walked past her discarded towel for her white robe, wondering why she bothered when she was thinking of joining him in the shower. She wanted to touch him, to close this distance that had arisen so abruptly between them.

"That," he agreed. "And we'll only be together for a short time. Call me your lover if you want to, but do not expect us to fall in love. Keep your expectations low."

She fell back a step as she tied her robe, giving it a firm yank like the action could tie off the wound he'd just inflicted.

But what did she think they were doing? Like fine weather, they were enjoying each other because they were here. That was all.

"I wasn't fishing for a marriage proposal," she defended.

"So long as we're clear." He aimed the remote and started the shower jets.

Scanning his stiff shoulders, she said, "Is this because I asked about your back? I'm sorry if that was too personal, but I've told you some really personal things about me."

"Talk to me about whatever you want. If I don't want to tell you something, I won't." He spoke with aloof confidence, but his expression faltered briefly, mouth quirking with self-deprecation.

Because he had already shared more than made him comfortable?

"There's nothing wrong with being friends, is there?"

He glanced at her, his expression patient, but resolute.

"You don't have friends," she recalled from the other night, thinking, *I can see why.* "What's wrong with friendship? Don't you want someone you can confide in? Share jokes with?"

His rebuff was making her feel like a houseguest who had to be tolerated. Surely they were past that! He'd just enjoyed *her* hospitality, hadn't he?

"They're cigar burns," he said abruptly, rattling the remote control onto the space behind the sink. "I have more on the bottoms of my feet. My captors used to make me scream so my grandfather could hear it over the phone. *There was more than one call.* Is that the sort of confiding you're looking for, Viveka?" he challenged with antagonism.

"Mikolas." Her breath stung like acid against the back of her throat. She unconsciously clutched the robe across her shattered heart.

"That's why I don't want to share more than our bodies. There's nothing else worth sharing."

Mikolas had been hard on Viveka this morning, he knew that. But he'd been the victim of forces greater than himself once before and already felt too powerless around her. The way she had infiltrated his life, the changes he was making for her, were unprecedented.

Earlier that day, he had risen while she slept and spent the morning sparring, trying to work his libido into exhaustion. She had to be sore. He wasn't an animal.

But one glance at her rising from the bath and all his command over himself had evaporated. At one point, he'd been quite sure he was prepared to beg.

Begging was futile. He *knew* that.

But so was thinking he could treat Viveka like every other woman he'd slept with. Many of them had asked about his back. He'd always lied, claiming chicken pox had caused the scars. For some reason, he didn't want to lie to Viveka.

When he had finally blurted out the ugly truth, he'd seen something in her expression that he outwardly rejected, but inwardly craved: agony on his behalf. Sadness for that dark time that had stolen his innocence and left him with even bigger scars that no one would ever see.

Damn it, he was self-aware enough to know he used denial as a coping strategy, but there was no point in raking over the coals of what had been done to him. Nothing would change it. Viveka wanted a jocular companion to share opinions and anecdotes with. He was never going to be that person. There was too much gravity and anger in him.

So he had schooled her on what to expect, and it left him sullen through the rest of the day.

She wasn't much better. In another woman, he would have called her subdued mood passive-aggressive, but he already knew how sensitive Viveka was under all that bravado. His churlish behavior had tamped down her natural cheerfulness. That made him feel even more disgusted with himself.

Then his grandfather asked her to play backgammon and she brightened, disappearing for a couple of hours, coming back to the penthouse only to change for the gym.

Why did that annoy him? He wanted her to be self-sufficient and not look to him to keep her amused. Later that evening, however, when he found her plumping cushions in the lounge, he had to ask, "What are you doing?"

"Tidying up." She carried a teacup and plate to the dumbwaiter and left it there.

"I pay people to do that."

"I carry my weight," she said neutrally.

He pushed his hands into his pockets, watching her click on a lamp and turn off the overhead light, then lift a houseplant—honest to God, she checked a plant to see if it needed water rather than look at him.

"You're angry with me for what I said this morning."

"I'm not." She sounded truthful and folded her arms defensively, but she finally turned and gave him her attention. "I just never wanted to be in this position again."

The bruised look in her eye made him feel like a heel.

"What position?" he asked warily.

"Being forced on someone who doesn't really want me around." Her tight smile came up, brave, but fatalistic.

"It's not like that," he ground out. "I told you I want you." Admitting it still made him feel like he was being hung by his feet over a ledge.

"Physically," she clarified.

Before the talons of a deeper truth had finished digging into his chest, she looked down, voice so low he almost didn't hear her.

"So do I. That's what worries me," she continued.

"What do you mean?"

She hugged herself, shrugging. Troubled. "Not something worth sharing," she mumbled.

Share, he wanted to demand, but that would be hypocritical. Regret and apology buzzed around him like biting mosquitoes, annoying him.

It had taken him years to come to this point of being completely sure in himself. A few days with this woman, and he was second-guessing everything he was or had or did.

"Can we just go to bed?" Her doe eyes were so vulnerable, it took a moment for him to comprehend what she was saying. He had thought they were fighting.

"Yes," he growled, opening his arms. "Come here."

She pressed into him, her lips touching his throat. He sighed as the turmoil inside him subsided.

Every night, they made love until Viveka didn't even remember falling asleep, but she always woke alone.

Was it personal? she couldn't help wondering. Did Mikolas not see anything in her to like? Or was he simply that removed from the normal needs of humanity that he genuinely didn't want any closer connections? Did he realize his behavior was hurtful? Did he know and not *care*?

Whenever she had dreamed of being in an intimate relationship with a man, it had been intimacy across the board, not this heart-wrenching openness during sex and a deliberate distance outside of it. Was she saying too much? *Asking* too much?

She became hypersensitive to every word she

spoke, trying to refrain from getting too personal. The constant weighing and worrying was exhausting.

It was harder when they traveled. At least with his grandfather at the table, the conversation flowed more naturally. As Mikolas dragged her to various events across Europe, she had to find ways to talk to him without putting herself out there too much.

"I might go to the art gallery while you're in meetings this morning. Unless you want to come? I could wait until this afternoon," was a typical, neutral approach. She loved spending time with him, but couldn't say *that*.

"I can make myself available after lunch."

"It's an exhibition of children's art," she clarified. "Is that something you'd want to see?" Now she felt like she was prying. Her belly clenched as she awaited rejection.

He shrugged, indifferent. "Art galleries aren't something I typically do, but if you want to see it, I'll take you."

Which made her feel like she was imposing on his time, but he was already tapping it into his schedule. Later he paced around the place, not saying much, while she held back asking what he thought. She wanted to tell him about her early aspirations and point to what she liked and ask if he'd ever messed around with finger paints as a child.

She actually found herself speaking more freely to strangers over cocktails than she did with him. He always listened intently, but she didn't know if that was for show or what. If he had interest in her thoughts or ambitions, she kept thinking, he would ask her himself, but he never did.

Tonight she was revealing her old fascination with art history and Greek mythology. It felt good to open up, so she shared a little more than she normally would.

"I actually won an award," she confided with a wrinkle of her nose. "It was just a little thing for a watercolor I painted at school. I was convinced I'd become a world-famous artist," she joked. "I've always wanted to take a degree in art, but there's never been the right time."

It was small talk. They were nice people, owners of a hotel chain whom she'd met more than once.

Deep down, she was congratulating herself on performing well at these events, remembering the names of children and occasionally going on shopping dates. Tonight she had found herself genuinely interested in Adara Makricosta's plans for her hotels. That's how her own career goals had come up. Adara Makricosta was the CEO of a family-owned chain and had asked Viveka about her own work.

Viveka sidestepped the admission she was merely a mistress whose job it was to create this warming trend Mikolas was enjoying among the world's most rich and powerful.

"Why didn't you tell me that before?" Mikolas asked when Adara and Gideon had moved on. "About wanting to study art," he prompted when she only looked at him blankly.

Viveka's heart lurched and she almost blurted out, *Because you wouldn't care*. She swallowed.

"It's not practical. I thought about taking evening classes around my day job, but I always had Hildy to look after. And I knew once I was in this position, looking to my own future, I would need to devote myself to a proper career, not dabble in something that will never pay the bills."

She ought to be thinking harder about that, not using up all her brain space trying to second-guess the man in front of her.

"You don't have bills now. Sign up for something," he said breezily.

"Where? To what end?" Her throat tightened. "We're constantly on the move and I don't know how long I'll be with you. No. There's no point." It would hurt to see that phoenix of a dream rise up from the ashes only to fly away.

Or was he implying she would be with him for the long term?

She did the unthinkable and searched his expression for some sign that he had feelings for her. That they had a future.

He receded behind a remote mask, horribly quiet for the rest of the night and even while they traveled back to Greece, adding an extra layer of tension to their trip.

Viveka was still smarting over Mikolas's behavior when she woke in his bed the next morning. They were sleeping late after arriving in the wee hours. She stayed motionless, naked in the spoon of his body, not wanting to move and wake him. She often fell asleep in his arms, but she never woke in them. This was a rare moment of closeness.

It was the counterfeit currency that all women—like mother like daughter—too often took in place of real regard.

Because, no matter how distanced she felt from Mikolas during the day, in bed she felt so integral to him it was a type of agony to be anywhere else. When he made love to her, it felt like love. His kisses and caresses were generous, his compliments extravagant. She warmed and tingled just thinking about how good it felt to join with him, but it wasn't just physical pleasure for her. Lying with him, naked and intimate, was emotionally fulfilling.

She was falling for him.

His breathing changed. He hardened against her backside and she bit her lip, heartened by the lazy stroke of his hand and the noise of contentment he made, like he was pleased to wake with her against him.

Such happiness brimmed in her, she couldn't help but wriggle her butt into his hardness, inviting the only affection he seemed to accept, wanting to hold on to this moment of harmony.

His mouth opened on her shoulder and his hand drifted down her belly into the juncture of her thighs. He made a satisfied noise when he found her wet and ready.

She gasped, stimulated by his lazy touch. She

stretched her arm to the night table, then handed a condom over her shoulder as she nestled back against him, eager and needy. He adjusted her position and a moment later thrust in, sighing a hot breath against her neck, setting kisses against her nape that were warm and soft. Caring. Surely he cared?

She took him so easily now. It was nothing but pleasure, so much pleasure. She hadn't known her body could be like this: buttery and welcoming. It was almost too good. She was so far ahead of him, having been thinking about this while he slept against her, she soared over the top in moments. She cried out, panting and damp with sweat, overcome and floating, speechless in her orgasmic bliss.

"Greedy," he said in a gritty morning voice, rubbing his mouth against her skin, inhaling and calling her beautiful in Greek. Exquisite. Telling her how much he enjoyed being inside her. How good she made him feel.

He came up on his elbow so he could thrust with more power. His hand went between her legs again, ensuring her pleasure as he moved with more aggression.

She didn't mind his vigor. She was so slick, still so aroused, she reveled in the slap of his hips into her backside, hand knotting in the bottom sheet to brace herself to receive him, making noises close to desperation as she felt a fresh pinnacle hover within reach.

"Don't hold back," he ground out. "Come with me. *Now.*"

He pounded into her, the most unrestrained he'd

ever been. She cried out as her excitement peaked. An intense climax rolled through her, leaving her shattered and quaking in ecstasy.

He convulsed with equal strength, arms caging her, hoarse shout hot against her cheek. He jerked as she clenched, continuing to push deep so she was hit by wave after wave of aftershocks while he thrust firmly into her, like he was implanting his essence into her core.

As the sensual storm battered them, he remained pressed over her, crushing her beneath his heavy body. Finally, the crisis began to subside and he exhaled raggedly as he slid flat, his one arm under her neck bending so he could cradle her into his front. They were coated in perspiration. It adhered her back to his front and she could feel his heart still pounding unsteadily against her shoulder blade. Their legs were tangled, their bodies still joined, their breaths slowing to level.

It was the most beautifully imperfect moment of her life. She loved him. Endlessly and completely. But he didn't love her back.

Mikolas had visited hell. Then his grandfather had accepted him and he had returned to the real world, where there were good days and bad days. Now he'd found what looked like heaven and he didn't trust it. Not one little bit.

But he couldn't turn away from it—*from her*—either.

Not without feeling as though he was peeling away

his own skin, leaving him raw and vulnerable. He was a molting crab, losing his shell every night and rebuilding it every day.

This morning was the most profound deconstruction yet. He always tried to leave before Viveka woke so he wouldn't start his day impacted by her effect on him, but the sweet way she'd rubbed herself into his groin had undone him. She had gone from a tentative virgin to a sensual goddess capable of stripping him down to nothing but pure sensation.

How could he resist that? How could he not let her press him into service and give himself up to the joy of possessing her. It had been all he could do to hold back so she came with him. Because she owned him. Between the sheets, she completely owned him. Right now, all he wanted in life was to stay in this bed, with her body replete against his, her fingertips drawing light patterns on the back of his hand.

Don't *want*.

He made himself roll away and sit up, to prove himself master over whatever this thing was that threatened him in a way nothing else could.

She stayed inside him, though. In his body as an intoxicant, and in his head as an unwavering awareness. And because he was so attuned to her, he heard the barely discernible noise she made as he pushed to stand. It was a sniff. A lash. A cat-o'-nine-tails that scored through his thick skin into his soul.

He swung around and saw only the bow of her back, still curled on her side where he'd left her. He dropped his knee into the mattress and caught her shoulder, flattening her so he could see her face.

She gasped in surprise, lifting a hand to quickly try to wipe away the tears that stood in her eyes. Self-conscious agony flashed in her expression before she turned her face to hide it.

His heart fell through the earth.

"I thought you were with me." He spoke through numb lips, horrified with himself. He could have sworn she had been as passionately excited as he was. He had felt her slickness, the ripples of her orgasm. Was he kidding himself with how well he thought he knew her?

"You have to tell me if I'm being too rough," he insisted, his usual command buried in a choke of self-reproach.

"It's not that." Her expression spasmed with dismay. She pushed the back of her wrist across her eye, then brushed his hand off her shoulder so she could roll away and sit up. "I used to be so afraid of sex. Now I like it."

She rubbed her hands up and down her arms, the delicacy of her frame striking like a hammer between his eyes. Her nude body pimpled at the chill as she rose.

"I'm grateful," she claimed, turning to offer him a smile, but her lashes were still matted. "Take a bow. Let me know what I owe you."

Those weren't tears of gratitude.

His heart lurched as he found himself right back in that moment where he had impulsively told her to pursue her interests and she had searched for reassurance that she would be with him for the long haul.

I don't know how long I'll be with you.

It had struck him at that moment that at some point she would leave and he hadn't been able to face it. He skipped past it now, only saying her name.

"Viveka." It hurt his throat. "I told you to keep your expectations low," he reminded, and felt like a coward, especially when her smile died.

She looked at him with betrayal, like he'd smacked her.

"Don't," he bit out.

"Don't what? Don't like it?"

"Don't be hurt." He couldn't bear the idea that he was hurting her. "Don't feel *grateful*."

She made a choking noise. "Don't tell me what to feel. That is where you control what I feel." She pointed at the rumpled sheets he knelt upon, then tapped her chest and said on a burst of passion, "In here? This is mine. I'll feel whatever the hell I want."

Her blue eyes glowed with angry defiance, but something else ravaged her. Something sweet and powerful and pure that shot like an arrow to pierce his breastbone and sting his heart. He didn't try to put a name to it. He was afraid to, especially when he saw shadows of hopelessness dim her gaze before she looked away.

"I'm not confusing sex with love, if that's what you're worried about." She moved to the chair and pulled on his shirt from the night before, shooting her arms into it and folding the front across her stomach. She was hunched as though bracing for body blows. "My mother made that mistake." Her voice was scuffed and desolate. "I won't. I know the difference."

Why did that make him clench his fist in despair? He ought to be reassured.

He almost told her this wasn't just sex. When he walked into a room with her hand in his, he was so proud it was criminal. When she dropped little tidbits about her life before she met him, he was fascinated. When she looked dejected like that, his armored heart creaked and rose on quivering legs, anxious to show valor in her name.

Instead he stood, saying, "I'll send an email today. To ask how the investigation is coming along. On your mother," he clarified, when she turned a blank look on him.

She snorted, sounding disillusioned as she muttered, "Thanks."

"Your head is not in the game today," Erebus said, dragging Viveka's mind to the *távli* board, where he was placing one of his checkers on top of hers.

Were they at *plakoto* already? Until a few weeks ago, she hadn't played since she and Trina were girls, but the rules and strategies had come back to her very quickly. She sat down with Erebus at least once a day if she was home.

"Jet lag," she murmured, earning a *tsk*.

"We don't lie to each other in this house, *poulaki mou*."

Viveka was growing fond of the old man. He was very well-read, kept up on world politics and had a wry sense of humor. At the same time, he was interested in *her*. He called her "my little birdie" and always had something nice to say. Today it had been, *"I wish you weren't leaving for Paris. I miss you when you're traveling."*

She'd never had a decent father figure in her life and knew it was crazy to see this former criminal in that light, but he was also sweetly protective of her. It was endearing.

So she didn't want to offend him by stating that his grandson was tearing her into little pieces.

"I wonder sometimes what Mikolas was like as a child," she prevaricated.

She and Erebus had talked a little about her aunt and he'd shared a few stories from his earliest years. She was deeply curious how such a kind-seeming man could have broken the law and fathered an infamous criminal, but thought it better not to ask.

He nodded thoughtfully, gesturing for her to shake the cup with the dice and take her turn.

She did and set the cup within his reach, but he was staring across the water from their perch outside his private sitting room. In a few weeks it would be too hot to sit out here, but it was balmy and pleasant today. A light breeze moved beneath the awning, carrying his favorite *kantada* folk music with it.

"Pour us an ouzo," he finally said, two papery fingers directing her to the interior of his apartment.

"I'll get in trouble. You're only supposed to have one before dinner."

"I won't tell if you don't," he said, making her smile.

He came in behind her as she filled the small glasses. He took his and canted his head for her to follow him.

She did, slowly pacing with him as he shuffled his cane across his lounge and into his bedroom. There he sat with a heavy sigh into a chair near the window. He picked up the double photo frame on the side table and held it out to her.

She accepted it and took her time studying the black-and-white photo of the young woman on the one side, the boy and girl sitting on a rock at a beach in the other. They were perhaps nine and five.

"Your wife?" she guessed. "And Mikolas's father?"

"Yes. And my daughter. She was... Men always say they want sons, but a daughter is life and light. A way for your wife to live on. Daughters are love in its purest form."

"That's a beautiful thing to say." She wished she knew more about her own father than a few barely recollected facts from her mother. He'd been English and had dropped out of school to work in radio. He'd married her mother because she was pregnant and died from a rare virus that had got into his heart.

She sat on the foot of Erebus's bed, facing him. "Mikolas told me you lost your daughter when she was young. I'm sorry."

He nodded, taking back the frame and looking at it

again. "My wife, too. She was beautiful. She looked at me the way you look at Mikolas. I miss that."

Viveka looked into her drink.

"I failed them," Erebus continued grimly. "It was a difficult time in our country's history. Fear of communism, martial law, censorship, persecution. I was young and passionate, courting arrest with my protests. I left to hide on this island, never thinking they would go after my wife."

His cloudy gray eyes couldn't disguise his stricken grief.

"The way my son told me, my daughter was crying, trying to cling to their mother as the military police dragged her away for questioning. They knocked her to the ground. Her ear started bleeding. She never came to. Brain injury, perhaps. I'll never know. My wife died in custody, but not before my son saw her beaten unconscious for trying to go back to our daughter."

Viveka could only cover her mouth, holding back a cry of protest.

"By the time I was reunited with him, my son was twisted beyond repair. I was warped, too. The law? How could I have regard for it? What I did then, bribes, theft, smuggling... None of that sits on my conscience with any great weight. But what my son turned into..."

He cleared his throat and set the photo frame back in its place. His hands shook and he took a long time to speak again.

"My son lost his humanity. The things he did...

I couldn't make him stop, couldn't bring him back from that. It was no surprise to me that he was killed so violently. It was the way he lived. When he died I mourned him, but I also mourned what should have been. I was forced to face my many mistakes. The things I had done caused me to outlive my children. I hated the man I had become."

His pain was tangible. Viveka ached for him.

"Into this came a ransom demand. A street rat was claiming to be my grandson. Some of my son's rivals had him."

Her heart clenched. She was listening intently, but was certain she wouldn't be able to bear hearing this.

"You want to know what Mikolas was like as a child? So do I. He came to me as an empty shell. Eyes this big." He made a circle with his finger and thumb. "Thin. Brittle. His hand was crushed, some of his fingernails gone. Three of his teeth gone. He was *broken*." He paused, lined face working to control deep pain, then he admitted, "I think he hoped I would kill him."

She bit her lip, eyes hot and wet, a burn of anguish like a pike spreading from her throat to the pit of her stomach.

"He said that if the blood test hadn't been positive, you wouldn't have helped him." She couldn't keep the accusation, the blame, out of her voice.

"I honestly can't say what I would have done," Erebus admitted, eyes rheumy. "Looking back from the end of my life, I want to believe my conscience would have demanded I help him regardless, but I wasn't much of a man at the time. They showed me a picture and he looked a little like my son, but..."

His head hung heavy with regret.

"He begged me to believe he was telling the truth, to accept him. I took too long." He took a healthy sip of his ouzo.

She'd forgotten she was holding one herself. She sipped, thinking how forsaken Mikolas must have felt. No wonder he was so impermeable.

"He thinks I want him to redeem the Petrides name, but *I* need redemption. To some extent I have it," Erebus allowed with deep emotion. "I'm proud of all he's accomplished. He's a good man. He told me why he brought you here. He did the right thing."

She suppressed a snort. Mikolas's reasons for keeping her and her reasons for staying were so fraught and complex, she didn't see any way to call them wholly right or wrong.

"He has never recovered his heart, though. All the things he has done? It hasn't been for me. He has built this fortress around himself for good reason. He trusts no one, relies on no one."

"Cares about no one," she murmured despondently.

"Is that what puts that hopeless expression on your face, *poulaki mou*?"

She knocked back her drink, giving a little shiver as the sweet heat spread from her tongue to the tips of her limbs. Shaking back her hair, she braced herself and said, "He'll never love me, will he?"

Erebus didn't bother to hide the sadness in his eyes. Because they didn't lie to each other.

Slowly the glow of hope inside her guttered and doused.

"We should go back to our game," he said.

CHAPTER TWELVE

MIKOLAS GLANCED UP as Viveka came out of the elevator. She never used it unless she was coming from the gym, but today she was dressed in the clothes she'd worn to lunch.

She staggered and he shot to his feet, stepping around his desk to hurry toward her. "Are you all right?"

"Fine." She set a hand on the wall, holding up the other to forestall him. "I just forgot that ouzo sneaks up on you like this."

"You've been *drinking*?"

"With your grandfather. Don't get mad. It was his idea, but I'm going to need a nap before dinner. That's what he was doing when I left him."

"This is what you two get up to over backgammon?" He took her arm, planning to help her to her room.

"Not usually, no." Her hand came to his chest. She didn't move, just stared at her hand on his chest, mouth grave, brow wearing a faint pleat. "We were talking."

That sounded ominous. She glanced up and anguish edged the blue of her irises.

Instinctively, he swallowed. His hand unconsciously tightened on her elbow, but he took a half step back from her. "What were you talking about?"

"He loves you, you know." Her mouth quivered, the corners pulling down. "He wishes you could forgive him."

He flinched, dropping his hand from her arm.

"He understands why you can't. Even if you did reach out to him, I don't think he would forgive himself. It's just…sad. He doesn't know how to reach you and—" She rolled to lean her shoulders against the wall, swallowing. "You won't let anyone in, ever, will you? Is this really all you want, Mikolas? Things? Sex without love?"

He swore silently, lifting his gaze to the ceiling, hands bunching into fists, fighting a wave of helplessness.

"I lied to you," he admitted when he trusted his voice. "That first day we met, I said my grandfather gave me anything I wanted." He lowered his gaze to her searching one. "I didn't want any of those things I asked for."

He had her whole attention.

"It was my test for him." He saw now the gifts had been his grandfather's attempts to earn his trust, but then it had been a game. A deadly, terrifying one. "I asked him for things I didn't care about, to see if he would get them for me. I never told him what I really wanted. I never told anyone."

He looked at his palm, rubbed one of the smooth

patches where it had been held against a hot kettle, leaving shiny scar tissue.

"I never tell anyone. Physical torture is inhuman, but psychological torture…" His hand began shaking.

"Mikolas." Her hand came into his. He started to pull away, but his fingers closed over hers involuntarily, holding on, letting her keep him from sinking into the dark memories.

His voice felt like it belonged to someone else. "They would ask me, 'Do you want water?' 'Do you want the bathroom?' 'Do you want us to stop?' Of course I said yes. They never gave me what I wanted."

Her hand squeezed his and her small body came into the hollow of his front, warm and anxious to soothe, arms going around his stiff frame.

He set his hands on her shoulders, resisting her offer of comfort even though it was all he wanted, ever. He resisted *because* it was what he wanted beyond anything.

"I can't—I'm not trying to hurt him. But if I trust him, if I let him mean too much to me, then what? He's not in a position to be my savior again. He's a weakness to be used against me. I can't leave myself open to that. Can you understand that?"

Her arms around him loosened. For a moment her forehead rested in the center of his chest, then she pressed herself away.

"I do." She took a deep, shaken breath. "I'm going to lie down."

He watched her walk away while two tiny, damp stains on his shirt front stayed cold against his skin.

* * *

"Vivi!" Clair exclaimed as she approached with her husband, Aleksy.

Viveka found a real smile for the first time all night. In days, really. Things between her and Mikolas were more poignantly strained than ever. She loved him so much and understood now that he was never going to let himself love her.

"How's the dress?" Viveka teased, rallying out of despondency for her hostess.

"I've taken to carrying a mending kit." Clair ruefully jiggled her pocketbook.

"I've been looking forward to seeing you again," Viveka said sincerely. "I've had a chance to read up on your foundation. I'm floored by all you do! And I have an idea for a fund-raiser that might work for you."

Mikolas watched Viveka brighten for the first time in days. Her smile caused a pang in his chest that was more of a gong. He wanted to draw that warmth and light of hers against the echoing discord inside him, finally settling it.

"I saw a children's art exhibit when we were in New York. I was impressed by how sophisticated some of it was. It made me think, what if some of your orphans painted pieces for an auction? Here, let me show you." She reached into her purse for her phone, pausing to listen to something Clair was saying about another event they had tried.

Beside him, Aleksy snorted.

Mikolas dragged his gaze off Viveka, lifting a cool brow of inquiry. He had let things progress naturally between the women, not pursuing things on the business front, willing to be patient rather than rush fences and topple his opportunity with the standoff-ish Russian.

"I find it funny," Aleksy explained. "You went to all this trouble to get my attention, and now you'd rather listen to her than speak to me. I made time in my schedule for you tomorrow morning, if you can tear yourself away…?"

Mikolas bristled at the supercilious look on the other man's face.

Aleksy only lifted his brows, not intimidated by Mikolas's dark glare.

"When we met in Athens, I wondered what the hell you were doing with her. What *she* was doing with *you*. But…" Aleksy's expression grew self-deprecat-ing. "It happens to the best of us, doesn't it?"

Mikolas saw how he had neatly painted himself into a corner. He could dismiss having any regard for Viveka and undo all her good work in getting him this far, or he could suffer the assumption that he had a profound weakness: *her.*

Before he had to act, Viveka said, "Oh, my God," and looked up from her phone. Her eyes were like dinner plates. "Trina has been trying to reach me. Grigor had a heart attack. He's dead."

Mikolas and Viveka left the party amid expressions of sympathy from Clair and Aleksy.

Viveka murmured a distracted "thank you," but they were words that sat on air, empty of meaning.

She was in shock. Numb. She wasn't *glad* Grigor was dead. Her sister was too torn up about the loss when she rang her, expressing regret and sorrow that a better relationship with her father would never manifest. Viveka wouldn't wish any sort of pain on her little sister, but she felt nothing herself.

She didn't even experience guilt when Mikolas surmised that Grigor had been under a lot of stress due to the inquiries Mikolas had ordered. He hadn't had much to report the other day, but ended a fresh call to the investigator as they returned to the hotel.

"The police on the island were starting to talk. They could see that silence looked like incompetence at best, bribery and collusion at worst. Charges were sounding likely for your mother's murder and more. My investigator is preparing a report, but without a proper court case, you'll probably never have the absolute truth on how she died. I'm sorry."

She nodded, accepting that. It was enough to know Grigor had died knowing he hadn't got away with his crimes.

"Trina will need me." It felt like she was stating the obvious, but it was the only concrete thought in her head. "I need to book a flight."

"I've already messaged my pilot. He's doing his preflight right now. We'll be in the air as soon as you're ready."

She paused in gathering the things that had been unpacked into drawers for her.

"Didn't I hear Aleksy say something about holding an appointment for you tomorrow?" She looked at the clothes she'd brought to Paris. "Not one thing suitable for a funeral," she murmured. "Would Trina understand if I wore that red gown, do you think?" She pointed across the room to the open closet.

No response from Mikolas.

She turned her head.

He looked like he was trying to drill into her head with his silvery eyes. "I can rebook with Aleksy."

So careful. So watchful. His remark about coming with her penetrated.

"Do you need to talk to Trina?" she asked, trying to think through the pall of details and decisions that would have to be made. "Because she inherits? Does his dying affect the merger?"

Something she couldn't interpret flickered across his expression. "There will be things to discuss, yes, but they can wait until she's dealt with immediate concerns."

"I wonder if he even kept her in his will," she murmured, setting out something comfortable to travel in, then pulling off her earrings. Gathering her hair, she moved to silently request he unlatch the sapphire necklace he'd given her this evening. "Trina told me he blamed me for everything, not her, so I hope he didn't disinherit her. Who else would he leave his wealth to? Charity? Ba-ha-ha. Not."

The necklace slithered away and she fetched the velvet box, handing it to him along with the earrings, then wormed her way out of her gown.

"Trina better be a rich woman, after everything he put her through. It doesn't seem real." She knew she was babbling. She was processing aloud, maybe because she was afraid of what *would* be said if she wasn't already doing the talking. "I've never been able to trust the times when I've thought I was rid of him. Even after I was living with Hildy, things would come up with Trina and I'd realize he was still a specter in my life. I was so sure the wedding was going to be *it*. Snip, snip, snip."

She made little scissors with her fingers, cutting ties to her stepfather, then bounced her butt into the seat of her jeans and zipped. Her push-up bra was overkill, but she pulled a T-shirt over it, not bothering to change into a different one.

"Now it's really here. He's dead. No longer able to wreck my life."

She made herself face him. Face *it*. The truth she had been avoiding.

"I'm finally safe from him."

Which meant Mikolas had no reason to keep her.

Mikolas was a quick study, always had been. He had seen the light of the train coming at him from the end of the tunnel the moment her lips had shaped the words, *He's dead*.

He had watched her pack and change and had listened to her walk herself to the platform and he still wasn't ready when her pale, pale face tilted up to his to say goodbye.

I can rebook with Aleksy. That was as close as he could come to stating that he was willing to continue their affair. He wasn't offering her solace. She wasn't upset beyond concern for her sister. God knew she didn't need *him*. He had deliberately stifled that expectation in her.

She looked down so all he could see of her expression was her pleated brow. "If you could give me some time to work out how to manage things with Aunt Hildy—"

He turned away, instantly pissed off. *So* pissed off. But he was unable to blame anyone but himself. He was the one who had fought letting ties form between them. He'd called what they had chemistry, sexual infatuation, protection.

"We're square," he growled. "Don't worry about it."

"Hardly. I'll get her house on the market as soon as I can—"

"I have what I wanted," he insisted, while a voice in his head asked, *Do you?* "I'm in," he continued doggedly. "None of the contacts I've made can turn their backs on me now."

"Mikolas—" She lowered to the padded bench in front of the vanity, inwardly quailing. *Don't humiliate yourself*, she thought, but stumbled forward like a love-drunk fool. "I care for you." Her voice thickened. "A lot." She had to clear her throat and swallow. Blink. Her fingers were a tangled mess against her knees. "If you would prefer we stay together...just say it. I know that's hard for you, but..." She warily lifted her gaze.

He was a statue, hands fisted in his pockets, immobile. Unmoved.

Her heart sank. "I can't make an assumption. I would feel like I'm still something you took on. I have to be something…" *You want.* Her mouth wouldn't form the words. This was hopeless. She could see it.

Mikolas's fists were so tight he thought his bones would crack. The shell around his heart was brittle as an egg's, threatening to crack.

"It's never going to work between us," he said, speaking as gently as he could, trying so hard not to bruise her. "You want things that I don't. Things I can't give you." He was trying to be *decent*, but he knew each word was a splash of acid. He felt the blisters forming in his soul. "It's better to end it here."

It happens to the best of us.

What about the worst? What about the ones who pushed it away before they knew what they were refusing?

What about the ones who were afraid because it meant succumbing to something bigger than themselves? Because it meant handing someone, *everyone*, the power to hurt him?

The room seemed to dim and quiet.

She nodded wordlessly, lashes low. Her gorgeous, kissable mouth pursed in melancholy.

And when she was gone, he wondered why, if the threat of Grigor was gone, he was still so worried about her. If he feared so badly that she would hurt him, why was her absence complete agony?

If all he had wanted from her was a damned business contact, why did he blow off his appointment with Aleksy the next morning and sit in a Paris hotel room all day, staring at sapphire jewelry he'd bought because the blue stones matched her eyes, willing his phone to ring?

"You're required to declare funds over ten thousand euros," the male customs agent in London said to Viveka as they entered a room that was like something off a police procedural drama. There was a plain metal table, two chairs, a wastebasket and a camera mounted in the ceiling. If there was a two-way mirror, she couldn't see it, but she felt observed all the same.

And exhausted. The charter from the island after Grigor's funeral had been delayed by weather, forcing her to miss her flight out of Athens. They had rebooked her, but on a crisscross path of whichever flight left soonest in the general direction of London. She hadn't eaten or slept and was positively miserable.

"I forgot I had it," she said flatly.

"You forgot you're carrying twenty-five thousand euros?"

"I was going to put it in the bank in Athens, but I had already missed my connection. I just wanted to get home."

He looked skeptical. "How did you come by this amount of cash?"

"My sister gave it to me. For my aunt."

His brows tilted in a way that said, *Right*.

She sighed. "It's a long story."

"I have time."

She didn't. She felt like she was going to pass out. "Can I use the loo?"

"No." Someone knocked and the agent accepted a file, glancing over the contents before looking at her with more interest. "Tell me about Mikolas Petrides."

"Why?" Her heart tripped just hearing his name. Instantly she was plunged into despair at having broken off with him. When she had left Paris, she had told herself her feelings toward Mikolas were tied up in his protecting her from Grigor, but as the miles between them piled up, she kept thinking of other things: how he'd saved her life. How he'd brought her a life jacket, and said all the right things that night in Athens. How he'd taught her to fight. And make love.

Tears came into her eyes, but now was not the time.

"It looks like you've been traveling with him," the agent said. "That's an infamous family to truck with."

"The money has nothing to do with him!" That was a small lie. Once Viveka had spilled to her sister how she had come to be Mikolas's mistress, Trina had gone straight to her father's safe and emptied it of the cash Grigor had kept there.

Use this for Hildy. She's my aunt, too. I don't want you in his debt.

Viveka had balked, secretly wanting the tie to Mikolas. Trina had accused her of suffering from Stockholm syndrome. Her sister had matured a lot with her marriage and the death of Grigor. She had actually invited Viveka to live with them, but Viveka didn't want to be in that house, on that island,

204 THE SECRET BENEATH THE VEIL

with newlyweds being tested by Trina's reversal of fortunes, since Grigor had indeed left Trina a considerable amount of money. Truth be told, Trina and Stephanos had a lot to work through.

So did Viveka. The two weeks with her sister had been enormously rejuvenating, but now it was time to finally, truly, take the wheel on her own life.

"Look." She sounded as ragged as she felt. "My half sister came into some money through the death of her father. My aunt is in a private facility. It's expensive. My sister was trying to help. That's all."

"Are you sure you didn't steal the money from Petrides? Because your flight path looks like a rabbit trying to outrun a fox."

"He wouldn't care if I did," she muttered, thinking about how generous he'd always been.

The agent's brows went up.

"I'm kidding! Don't involve him." All that work on his part—a lifetime of building himself into the head of a legitimate enterprise—and she was going to tumble it with one stupid quip? *Nice job, Viveka.*

"Tell me about your relationship with him."

"What do you mean?"

"You slept with him?"

"Yes. And no," she rushed on, guessing what he was going to say next. "Not for twenty-five thousand euros."

"Why did you break it off?"

"Reasons."

"Don't be smart, Ms. Brice. I'm your only friend right now. What was the problem? A lover's tiff?

And you helped yourself to a little money for a fresh start?"

"There was no tiff." He didn't love her. That was the tiff. He would never love her and *she loved him so much.* "I'm telling you, the money has nothing to do with him. *I* have nothing to do with him. Not anymore."

She was going to cry now, and completely humiliate herself.

Mikolas was standing at the head of a boardroom table when his phone vibrated.

Viveka's picture flashed onto the screen. It was a photo he'd taken stealthily one day when creeping up on her playing backgammon with his grandfather. He'd perfectly caught her expression as she'd made a strong play, excited triumph brightening her face.

"Where's Vivi?" his grandfather had asked when Mikolas returned from Paris without her.

"Gone."

Pappoús had been stunned. Visibly heartbroken, which had concerned Mikolas. He hadn't considered how Viveka's leaving would affect his grandfather.

Pappoús had been devastated for another reason. "Another broken heart on my conscience," he'd said with tears in his eyes.

"It's not your fault." *He* was the one who had forced her to stay with him. He'd seduced her and tried not to lead her on, but she'd been hurt all the same. "She liked you," he tried to mollify. "If anything, you gave her some of what I couldn't."

"No," his grandfather had said with deep emotion. "If I hadn't left you suffering, you would not be so damaged. You would be able to love her as she's meant to be loved."

The words stung, but they weren't meant to be cruel. The truth hurt.

"You have never forgiven me and I wouldn't deserve it if you did," Pappoús went on. "I allowed your father to become a monster. He gave you nothing but a name that put you through hell. That is my fault." His shaking fist struck his chest.

He was so white and anguished, Mikolas tensed, worried his grandfather would put himself into cardiac arrest.

"I wasn't a fit man to take you in, not when you needed someone to heal you," Pappoús declared. "My love came too late and isn't enough. You don't trust it. So you've rejected her. She doesn't deserve that pain and it comes back to me. It's my fault she's suffering."

Mikolas had wanted to argue that what Viveka felt toward him wasn't real love, but if anyone knew how to love, it was her. She loved her sister to the ends of the earth. She experienced every nuance of life at a level that was far deeper than he ever let himself feel.

"She'll find love," Mikolas had growled, and was instantly uncomfortable with the idea of another man holding her at night, making her believe in forever. He hated the invisible man who would make her smile in ways he never had, because she finally felt loved in return.

"Vivi is resilient," his grandfather agreed with poignant pride.

She was very resilient.

When Mikolas had received the final report on Grigor's responsibility for her mother's death, he had been humbled. The report had compiled dozens of reports of assault and other wrongdoings across the island, but it was the unearthed statement made by Viveka that had destroyed him.

How much difference was there between one man pulling his tooth and another bruising a girl's eye? Mikolas had lost his fingernails. Viveka had lost her *mother*. He had been deliberately humiliated, forced to beg for air and water—death even—until his DNA had saved him. She had made her way to a relative who hadn't wanted her and had kept enough of a conscience to care for the woman through a tragic decline.

Viveka would find love because, despite all she had endured, she was *willing* to love.

She wasn't a coward, ducking and weaving, running and hiding, staying in Paris, saying, *It's better that it ends here.*

It wasn't better. It was torment. Deprivation gnawed relentlessly at him.

But the moment her face flashed on his phone, respite arrived.

"I have to take this," Mikolas said to his board, voice and hand trembling. He slid his thumb to answer, dizzy with how just anticipating the sound of her voice eased his suffering. "Yes?"

"I thought I should warn you," she said with remorse. "I've kind of been arrested."

"Arrested." He was aware of everyone stopping their murmuring to stare. Of all the things he might have expected, that was the very last. But that was Viveka. "Are you okay? Where are you? What happened?"

Old instincts flickered, reminding him he was revealing too much, but in this moment he didn't care about himself. He was too concerned for her.

"I'm fine." Her voice was strained. "It's a long story and Trina is trying to find me a lawyer, but they keep bringing up your name. I didn't want to blindside you if it winds up in the papers or something. You've worked so hard to get everything just so. I hate to cast shadows. I'm really sorry, Mikolas."

Only Viveka would call to forewarn him and ask nothing for herself. How in the world had he ever felt so threatened by this woman?

"Where are you?" he repeated with more insistence. "I'll have a lawyer there within the hour."

CHAPTER THIRTEEN

Mikolas's lawyer left Viveka at Mikolas's London flat, since it was around the corner from his own. She was on her very last nerve and it was two in the morning. She didn't try to get a taxi to her aunt's house. She didn't have the key and would have to ask the neighbor for one tomorrow.

So she prevailed upon Mikolas *again* and didn't bother trying to find bedding for his guest room. She threw a huge pity party for herself in the shower, crying until she couldn't stand, then she folded Mikolas's black robe into a firm hug around her and crawled into his bed with a box of tissues that she dabbed against her leaking eyes.

Sleep was her blessed escape from feeling like she'd only alienated him further with this stupid questioning. The customs agents were hanging on to the money for forty-eight hours, because they could, but the lawyer seemed to think they'd give it up after that. She really didn't care, she was just so exhausted and dejected and she missed Mikolas so bad…

A weight came onto the mattress beside her and

a warm hand cupped the side of her neck. The lamp came on as a man's voice said, "Viveka."

She jerked awake, sitting up in shock.

"Shh, it's okay," he soothed. "It's just me. I was trying not to scare you."

She clutched her hand across her heart. "What are you doing here?"

His image impacted her. Not just his natural sex appeal in a rumpled shirt and open collar. Not just his stubbled cheeks and bruised eyes. There was such tenderness in his gaze, her fragile composure threatened to crumple.

"Your lawyer said you were in Barcelona." She had protested against Mikolas sending the lawyer, insisting she was just informing him as a courtesy, but he'd got most of the story out of her before her time on the telephone had run out.

"I was." His hooded lids lowered to disguise what he was thinking and his tongue touched his lip. "And I'm sorry to wake you, but I didn't want to scare you if I crawled in beside you."

She followed his gaze to the crushed tissues littering the bed and hated herself for being so obvious. "I was being lazy about making up the other bed. I'll go—"

"No. We need to talk. I don't want to wait." He tucked her hair back from her cheek, behind her ear. "Vivi."

"Why did you just call me that?" She searched his gaze, her brow pulled into a wrinkle of uncertainty, her pretty bottom lip pinched by her teeth.

"Because I want to. I have wanted to. For a long time." It wasn't nearly so unsettling to admit that as he'd feared. He had expected letting her into his heart would be terrifying. Instead, it was like coming home. "Everyone else does."

A tentative hope lit her expression. "Since when do you want to be like everyone else?"

He acknowledged that with a flick of his brow, but the tiny flame in his chest grew bigger and warmer.

"Since when do I tell you or anyone what I want? Is that what you're really wondering?" He wanted so badly to hold her. Gather all that healing warmth she radiated against him and close up the final gaps in his soul. He made himself give her what she needed first. "I want *you*, Vivi. Not just for sex, but for things I can't even articulate. That scares me to say, but I want you to know it."

She sucked in a breath and covered her mouth with both hands.

This can't be real, Viveka thought, blinking her gritty eyes. She pinched herself and he let out a husk of a laugh, immediately trying to erase the sting with a gentle rub of his thumb.

His hand stayed on her arm. His gaze lifted to her face while a deeply tender glow in his eyes went all the way through her to her soul.

"I was terrified that if I let myself care for you, someone would use that against me. So what did I do? I pushed you away and inflicted the pain on myself. I was right to fear how much it would hurt if you were out of my reach. It's unbearable."

"Oh, Mikolas." Her mouth trembled. "You inflicted it on both of us. I want to be with you. If you want me, I'm right here."

He gathered her up, unable to help himself. For a long time he held her, just absorbing the beauty of having her against him. He was aware of a tickling trickle on his cheek and dipped his head to dry his cheek against her hair.

"Thank you for saying you want me," she said. Her slender arms tightened until she pressed the breath from his lungs. "It's enough, you know." She lifted her red eyes to regard him. "I won't ask you to say you love me. But I should have said it myself before I left Paris. I've been sorry that I didn't. I was trying to protect myself from being more hurt than I was. It didn't work," she said ruefully. "I love you so much."

"You're too generous." He cupped her cheek, wiping away her tear track with the pad of his thumb, humbled. "I want your love, Vivi. I will pay any price for that. Don't let me be a coward. Make me give you what you need. Make me say it and mean it."

"You're not a coward." Fresh tears of empathy welled in her eyes, seeping into all those cracks and fissures around his heart, widening them so there was more room for her to come in.

"I was afraid to tell you I was coming," he admitted. "I was afraid you wouldn't be here if you knew. That you wouldn't let me try to convince you to stay with me."

Viveka's heart was pattering so fast she could hardly breathe. "You only have to ask," she reminded.

"Ask." Mikolas smoothed her hair back from her face, gazing at her, humbly offering his heart as a flawed human being. "I can't insult you by asking you to *stay* with me. I must ask you the big question. Will you be my wife?"

Viveka's heart staggered and lurched. "Are you serious?"

"Of course I'm serious!" He was offended, but wound up chuckling. "I will have the right woman under the veil this time, too. Actually," he added with a light kiss on her nose, "I did the first time. I just didn't know it yet."

Tears of happiness filled her eyes. She threw her arms around his neck, needing to kiss him then. To hold him and *love* him. "Yes. Of course I'll marry you!"

Their kiss was a poignant, tender reunion, making all of her ache. The physical sparks between them were stronger than ever, but the moment was so much more than that, imbued with trust and openness. It was expansive and scary and uncharted.

Beautiful.

"I want to make love to you," he said, dragging his mouth to her neck. "*Love*, Vivi. I want to wake next to you and make the best of every day we are given together."

"Me, too," she assured him with a catch of joy in her voice. "I love you."

EPILOGUE

"Papa, I'm cold."

Viveka heard the words from her studio. She was in the middle of a still life of Callia's toys for the advanced painting class she'd been accepted into. Three years of sketching and pastels, oils and watercolors, and she was starting to think she wasn't half bad. Her husband was always quick to praise, of course, but he was shamelessly biased.

She wiped the paint off her fingers before she picked up the small pink jumper her daughter had left there on the floor. When she came into the lounge, however, she saw that it was superfluous. Mikolas was already turning from his desk to scoop their three-year-old into his lap.

Callia stood on his thigh to curl her arms around his neck before bending her knees and snuggling into his chest, light brown curls tucked trustingly against his shoulder. "I love you," she told him in her high, doll-like voice.

"I love you, too," Mikolas said with the deep timbre of sincerity that absolutely undid Viveka every time she heard it.

"I love Leo, too," she said in a poignant little tone, mentioning her cousin, Trina's newborn son. She had cried when they'd had to come home. She looked up at Mikolas. "Do you love Leo?"

"He spit up on my new shirt," Mikolas reminded drily, then magnanimously added, "But yes, I do."

Callia giggled, then began turning it into a game. "Do you love Theítsa Trina?"

"I've grown very fond of her, yes."

"Do you love Theíos Stephanos?"

"I consider him a good friend."

"Did you love Pappoús?" She pointed at the photo on his desk.

"I did love him, very much."

Callia didn't remember her great-grandfather, but he had held her swaddled form, saying to Viveka, *She has your eyes*, and proclaiming Mikolas to be a very lucky man.

Mikolas had agreed wholeheartedly.

Losing Erebus had been hard for him. For both of them, really. Fortunately, they'd had a newborn to distract them. Falling pregnant had been a complete surprise to both of them, but the shock had quickly turned to excitement and they were so enamored with family life, they were talking of expanding it even more.

"Do you love Mama?" Callia asked.

Mikolas's head came up and he looked across at Viveka, telling her he'd been aware of her the whole time. His love for her shone like a beacon across the space between them.

"My love for your mother is the strongest thing in me."

* * * * *

If you enjoyed this story, check out these other great reads from Dani Collins
BOUGHT BY HER ITALIAN BOSS
THE CONSEQUENCE HE MUST CLAIM
THE MARRIAGE HE MUST KEEP
VOWS OF REVENGE
SEDUCED INTO THE GREEK'S WORLD
Available now!